No Vacancy

Anna Ellis

THREE BIRDS PRESS

No Vacancy

CHAPTER ONE

WILLIAM WATCHED THE GROUP in the bedroom.

The two-way mirror separated him from the activity, one of the many renovations he completed years ago. His private office led into the bedroom, the expansive space more for play than sleeping. Hidden speakers allowed him to hear every sound in the next room. He could close his eyes and visualize what was happening if he wanted to.

William preferred to watch.

He placed a hand on the glass, leaning closer. The men in the room weren't as skilled as he was. But the sound of the woman's scream tightened the smile on his face.

William had wanted a playroom; every toy and tool that could be used for pain and pleasure was found in the room. While William was skilled at providing both, he would admit that he enjoyed causing pain a bit more than pleasure.

His own private Red Room. He'd wanted a space where he could wield complete control and like always, William had gotten what he wanted.

Those using the room were required to do everything he demanded.

There were four of them in there now. The lithesome Serena lay on the bed, her wrists restrained in the padded cuffs. One of the men crouched between her legs, teasing her into a torment with a vibrator. Another knelt beside her, and as William watched avidly, he thrust his cock into Serena's mouth, holding her head with a firm grip.

The third man stood back and directed the action. He had no idea William was watching as well.

As William watched Serena's feeble tugs on her restraints, his thoughts turned to Iliya, whose excitement would quickly reach a fever pitch when he tied her up.

Iliya. How he adored her. In bed and out. There was nothing she wouldn't have let him do to her. Let anyone else do to her. She accepted it all, everything he had ever devised. Enjoyed it. Loved it.

He missed her. William had heard nothing from her in months, not since she'd run off with that writer of Morena's. William missed her, but he knew Iliya would come back to him. She always did. She would always submit to him.

Unlike Morena.

Now Morena had been one of his women who disliked to be tied up. If she did, it had to be on her terms. In all the years William had known her, in all the times they'd been together, Morena had never once submitted to him, not fully.

Maybe that was what kept drawing him back to her.

Iliya was a younger Morena, but without the spark. Iliya had a dangerous edge to her, one that suggested as much as she liked to be used, she'd always get the upper hand in return.

William's thoughts turned to the party downstairs. His friends had begun their play in his games room before he suggested they move upstairs. He had intended on joining them but had gotten caught up watching them instead.

Three other guests were still downstairs, caught up in their own devices. William enjoyed hosting parties, appreciated the adventurousness of his friends. They knew what was expected of them when they arrived at one of William's gatherings.

That they had been invited to entertain, to do whatever William wanted. However he wanted it.

If William wanted to see two women together, they would do it. If he wanted to fuck someone on his pool table, there would be a lineup before him waiting to take part. If he wanted a man to go down on his best friend, then it would happen.

If he wanted to watch a woman get tied up and used by three men...that was what he was watching.

William Burgess was rich and powerful and was in control of his world.

Serena screamed as she came, the sound piped into his office as clear as if he was in the room, her body writhing on the bed. It wasn't over. It had only begun, and there was plenty of time for William to join in.

He would go down to check on the others, before joining in the fun in the playroom. He knew what Serena liked, and her partners weren't providing it.

A sudden pain clutched at his heart.

He drew a shuddering breath. That was...no, it couldn't be? Heartburn or a pulled muscle...

The next pain was sharper and ripped the breath from his lungs. William's eyes widened, his mouth gaping. His hand slapped feebly against the window before he dropped to the floor.

CHAPTER TWO

Gemma

"I'VE BEEN THERE," CALLIE announced.

Gemma hoped the awe and admiration in her gaze weren't obvious to everyone. It was like having a crush on Brad Jacobson in eighth grade–she couldn't stop looking at him whenever he spoke, and even when he didn't.

It was like Gemma had a crush on Callie. A girl crush.

It had been that way since Callie had joined their Dirty Books Book Club, and now at their second meeting, it had gotten substantially worse.

"You've been to Halifax?" Gemma asked, willing to forgo her attempt to tell the others about Jasper's convention in Nova Scotia to listen to another one of Callie's stories. They were outrageous and somewhat over the top but Gemma wanted to hear everything about Callie's life. Callie had lived and loved–maybe not *loved* but certainly had slept with a variety of men.

It sounded like such fun to Gemma.

"It wasn't too far from Halifax. I went to this bed and breakfast for a weekend." Already Gemma could tell by the gleam in the woman's eyes that Callie was about to reveal something wildly inappropriate.

Not that Gemma was against inappropriate. Far from it. After all, wasn't that what this book club was about? To be able to read books with a little bit of spice? Steam? Sex that didn't involve incest or rape or some other life-altering, traumatic experience?

The four of them, Gemma, Nia, Emmy, and Malcolm, had decided to leave the book club they were in after Gemma requested an easier read.

"This was pretty heavy," she had said the last meeting, hefting her copy of *Moby Dick.*

"It's a classic." Penelope, the so-called "leader" of the club dismissed her with a sideways glance. Gemma had seen glances like that before and they never served to intimidate, only infuriate.

"It's a boring classic," Nia had said under her breath.

"You're in this club to enrich your mind and soul reading classic literature," Penelope proclaimed, with a sweep of her arm that almost took out her cup of tea.

Tea, not wine. What kind of book club met on a Thursday evening and served *tea?*

"I'm here to make friends," Emmy had said, meeting Gemma's gaze with a smile.

"What about that *Book Club* movie," Gemma said, staring at her book. "The one with Jane Fonda where they read *Fifty Shades of Grey.* What about reading something like that? There are so many good books out there."

"From this century," Nia muttered.

Apoplectic faces greeted Gemma's suggestions.

"We do not read works of that..." Penelope's mouth worked like she was a fish gasping for air as she searched for the right word. "Filth!"

"Garbage!"

"Smut."

"We just don't read such things," Penelope finished.

Gemma looked around. She'd been in the group for a year and a half, and the only thing she got from the books were the headaches from trying to read the small print. "Well, I do." She stood up. "So maybe I'll find another book club. Anyone feel like joining me, feel free."

Nia was right behind her, and then Emmy. And then, surprise of all surprises, Malcolm joined them.

Gemma was all about inappropriate. At least she wanted to be. She wanted to be more like Callie.

When Nia had asked about bringing her sister-in-law to the meetings, Gemma had agreed, thinking the mysterious in-law would be like Nia; long and lanky and a bit on the negative side.

Instead, the blond bombshell that was Callie erupted into the group, and Gemma's life was changed forever.

"I've never stayed in a bed and breakfast," Gemma admitted, leaning forward to pour herself more wine, this month's book selection still sitting untouched beside her. "Jasper likes having his own washroom when we stay someplace."

"The place I went to was a different sort of B & B." Callie paused before she bit into a spring roll. "It was for swingers."

Nia whipped around to glare at Callie with such force that Gemma suspected whiplash. "You're a swinger?!"

"I'm whatever you want me to be," Callie replied with a lazy smile. "In this place, couples and singles go and during dinner–although they also give you this awesome breakfast–people start hooking up. There's this guy there–Lorde." She gave a lascivious shiver. "So fine. It's a great place; so much fun. You should go there with your husband, Gemma."

Gemma shut her mouth which had been hanging open. "I–really? People go and have sex with each other? Just like that?"

Callie laughed and snagged another spring roll. She even held it suggestively before dipping it into the plum sauce. "There's a little more to than that. You talk to people, find out who attracts you, what they're into. You understand what swingers are, right?"

Gemma's face flushed. "Of course."

Even though she really didn't. She'd heard the word, had a vague understanding of the concept, but to actually meet a woman who referred to herself as a swinger was almost unbelievable. Didn't swingers wear leopard print, too-tight clothes and excessive make-up?

Emmy glanced at Gemma with wide eyes. "Really?"

"Not really," Gemma admitted. "I thought it was like couples who have sex with other couples in the same room, and they have parties with keys and orgies–"

"Sort of," Callie said.

"But you're not a couple." Gemma drew back. "I mean, you might be, but I was under the impression you weren't."

"I'm not one for monogamy." She held her glass out for Malcolm to pour her a refill of wine and winked her thanks. "Which makes me perfect for couples who want to change things up a bit. Add a friend."

"You...you do threesomes?" Emmy asked, eyes growing even wider.

Callie glanced at Nia, who was staring at her sister-in-law with an astonished expression and shrugged. "You said this book club was to widen horizons, find out what's out there. Well, I'm telling them so they don't have to do so much reading. Yes, I've done threesomes and foursomes and every other *somes* you can think of. It's fun."

Malcolm cleared his throat. "Fun."

Callie gave him a cheeky smile. "It can be. But back to the B & B; I think you should visit," she said to Gemma. "Couldn't hurt."

"It might," Nia muttered.

"Every marriage needs a little excitement," Callie continued, ignoring Nia. "You just have to find what you're into."

Gemma gave a shaky laugh as she reached for her wine. "I don't know if I'd be into that. Or Jasper."

"Could you do something like that?" Emmy pressed. Gemma couldn't tell what her friend was thinking. She'd known Emmy for a few years. She considered them good friends without getting too in-depth about serious subjects like marriage and sex.

The list of friends that Gemma could talk to about things like that was a big fat zero.

"I don't know."

Gemma was at a loss for what she wanted if anything. Her marriage was fine. Good. Great. She'd been in love with Jasper from the very first day she'd laid eyes on him at university. The math genius had been nothing like the boys from her tiny Western Ontario hometown. She was a country girl, through and through and had somehow ended up with city boy Jasper.

Gemma didn't regret Jasper one little bit, but after turning thirty a few months ago, she had begun to wonder about her lack of experience. She'd only known one man, and while Jasper satisfied her completely, she was beginning to wonder about what else was out there.

Callie didn't lack experience; Gemma could be sure of that.

"My wife was into that," Malcolm offered. Nia's head swivelled to stare at Malcolm. "Being a swinger. Since we're being open."

"I didn't think we were being that open," Nia muttered.

"Isn't that the whole point of reading these books?" Emmy pointed to her copy of *Outlander*. "So we can open up our sensuality?"

"That's what I signed up for." Callie helped herself to more wine, topping up Gemma's glass as well.

"I don't think you need much help," Gemma said weakly.

"Do you? You've been married how long? If you don't mind me asking."

Gemma didn't mind her asking but felt that Callie wouldn't care even if she did. Callie was the sort of woman who went after what, or whom, she wanted.

Gemma wanted to be that person.

"I don't think my marriage needs help. We've been together six years and things are still...fresh."

"Fresh, like a new loaf of bread, fresh? We're talking steamy, spicy. How are things in the bedroom? Would you go for a trip like this?" Callie grabbed her phone out of her bag and while Gemma was wondering how best to answer, quickly tapped out something. "Here." Callie passed her the phone.

Adults Only

Overlooking the Bay of Fundy in
picturesque Nova Scotia,
Mrs. Robinson's Bed and Breakfast
is the perfect spot to relax, to be refreshed and to reflect
on the adventure of life.

Emmy leaned over her shoulder. "Wow. But it doesn't say it's for swingers."

"Look down in the comments. Would you go to someplace like this?" Callie asked Emmy.

"In a minute," Emmy laughed. Callie turned to Malcolm.

"It might have helped my marriage," he admitted.

"But my marriage doesn't need help," Gemma pointed out.

"Everyone's marriage needs help," Nia said knowingly.

"You should call," Callie urged. "Since you'll already be in the area. Morena, the woman who runs the place, is amazing. She's over fifty and the sexiest woman I've ever met." She gave a catlike smile. "Which is saying a lot."

Gemma looked at Callie and glanced back at the phone again. The idea was intriguing, but the concept so foreign that Gemma wouldn't even know how to bring it up with Jasper. How would she possibly tell him she wanted to have sex with another man.

Or woman.

"I don't know what Jasper would say," she said finally, unwilling to commit. It was a big step just talking about it.

Callie shrugged. "Don't tell him."

CHAPTER THREE

Morena

MORENA SLAPPED HER HAND on Jed's chest as she rode him. Her white hair fell across her face and she pushed it back impatiently.

Jed cupped her breast. "God, you're beautiful when you do that." His eyes closed as he huffed out a breath, opened again to smile at her.

"Do what?" Morena had the rock and the rhythm down perfectly, setting the pace and speed, taking what she wanted from him.

"Fuck me like you do. I could watch you go all day."

"And I could do this all day." Morena slowed her frantic pace enough to rise up more, keeping the tip of Jed's cock inside before she impaled herself with a low cry.

"So could I. Which is why we're perfect together."

"If you say so." Talking was becoming difficult, especially as Morena fought to reach her peak. Knowing she was close, Jed reached between her to give her clit a casual rub. At her gasp, he continued, helping her along.

Morena tossed her head back, conscious only of the sensations running through her body. At the beautiful man under her, at his cock inside her. She loved his body, how he made her feel...she loved him...

Jed thrust up; once, twice to push Morena over the edge. She flew over the cusp with a cry, her body arching as she came. Jed clutched her hips, his fingers biting into her skin as he joined her.

Morena lay curled up against Jed, warm and snug against his body. Morena had never been one to cuddle before Jed, preferring to give and take her pleasure before leaving for the comfort of her own bed. But Jed gave her no choice, wanting to keep her close, to prolong the intimacy.

If he had his way, they would be living together by now.

Morena had never wanted to live with a thirty-eight-year-old, even when she had been thirty-eight. Now at fifty-six, Morena liked her own space, her routine and couldn't fathom the idea of changing things.

They had been together for a few months now, ever since Jed had come to her rescue when she had been dragged down to the police station for assault. It had been especially helpful that Jed had been there when the alleged assault had taken place. Thanks to Jed, the police quickly realized it had not been an assault, but only Morena defending herself against unwanted attention. She'd punched a potential date in the nose after he'd insulted her and gotten too handsy with her. When he'd slunk off, Morena had thought it had been the end of it.

But unfortunately, small minds in small towns did more talking than what was good for them. The recipient of her right hook was none other than a friend of Alan's, Elizabeth's manipulative husband.

Alan thought that by hurting Morena, it was a prime way to get revenge on Lorde for Elizabeth's defection. Morena would make sure he thought differently. And this time Morena wouldn't need Jed's help.

Jed lazily stroked her back, bringing her back to their cozy, warm nest. His house may not be much, spartan in décor with a man's sense of style, but his bed was one of the most comfortable Morena had ever had the pleasure of lying in. It was a giant, king-sized, with a carved wooden headboard that Morena had gripped more than once. His sheets were the best quality, his duvet, thick and warm. And the pillows...

If they ever made the step to live together, she would make sure he kept his bed.

She closed her eyes at the well of emotion surging within her.

She loved Jed. Was it time to tell him? Take the next step? It had been three months since they started seeing each other. Dating.

Having sex.

And the sex was incredible.

Morena had never known a man to be so in tune with her body. Jed knew what she wanted a moment before she did. He was considerate and giving and the stamina...

She was happy with him, but there was no way Morena was about to call Jed her boyfriend. The term seemed so juvenile to her ears.

"You still in there?" Jed murmured.

Morena sighed as she stretched against him. "Mm-hm. Just basking."

"I'm all for basking."

Silence between them, enough that Morena could hear Jed's heart beating, strong and true. Did he love her with that heart?

"Morena?" Something in Jed's voice caught her attention and she lifted her head. Was this it? Was he about to tell her how he felt? Could she? "About your next weekend here..."

Morena shifted away to pull the sheet over her bare breasts.

This didn't sound like true confession time.

They had been dancing around the issue of what went on at the inn for the entire time they'd been dating. Once a month, Morena hosted a weekend for like-minded couples and singles to enjoy each other.

Swingers weekends. She ran a bed and breakfast that catered to swingers.

Morena herself used to call herself a swinger. She'd been part of the community, happy with the lifestyle. There had been times during her marriages where she had pulled away, but there was something about the freedom and friendship of the community that kept drawing her back in.

But since Jed had come into her life, Morena had pulled away again. She still hosted the weekends but didn't take part in the after-dinner events. And she kept Jed separate from that part of her life.

So far.

"Which is next week," she said. "There are people coming next weekend."

"Which means no Morena for me this weekend," Jed added, the mournful tone in his voice making her smile. "Unless..."

Morena caught her breath. "Unless what?"

"Unless you wanted to play too."

Morena tucked her arm under her head and studied Jed. He was tanned year-round from working outside on his cranberry farm, and the way his blue eyes crinkled when he smiled was making lines at the corners of his eyes. It would age him, but not enough to catch up to Morena. She took a deep breath to push down the sense of foreboding. "Do you?"

Jed shrugged. In his last relationship, Jed had told Morena he'd had a friend who used to join him and his girlfriend. They had touched on his involvement in the swinger community, but since Jed had recently moved back to Nova Scotia from the States, their circles didn't overlap.

"Am I not enough for you?"

The question slid out in a whisper before Morena could stop it. She hadn't wanted to ask, didn't want to seem that vulnerable, needy or even insecure. But being with a younger man did strange things to her sometimes.

Jed hugged her close. "Don't be silly. That's not it and you know it. You're more than enough for me. I just thought, don't you miss it? Having someone new? Not that I don't love being with you."

"I know."

"Do you?"

Morena looked into his blue eyes, so serious for once. "Yes. I like what we have, Jed, and I hadn't thought of changing things."

Jed rolled onto his back. "Fair enough."

Morena mirrored his move and the two lay staring at the darkened ceiling, with the circle of light from the bedside lamp. The only sound in the room was the whisper of air breezing through the window. Morena needed a cool room and usually left the window open a crack to cool the room and her frequent hot flashes.

"It doesn't mean I hadn't thought of what it might be like."

Morena heard the rustle of sheets as Jed turned to glance at her. She stared straight up, not wanting to meet his gaze. "You being with another woman...I don't like the thought of it but..." She paused to collect her words. "I have to admit, it's kind of exciting to think about it. How you would touch her?"

"Like I touch you?" His hand ran along her hip, burrowed between her legs to cup her. Morena felt another surge of excitement. She couldn't get enough of Jed. "Would you want to watch something like that?"

"I'm not one for just watching, though."

"I'd like to watch you with another woman."

Morena heard the arousal in Jed's voice, shivered as he began to stroke her again with strong fingers. "What about another man?"

"I like to watch you come." The admission thrilled something deep inside Morena. "I'd rather it be me that made you come, but if there was to be anyone else with us, I'd want to watch. If you were okay with that."

"What about a swap, but in the same room?" Morena suggested, cringing at the technicality of the question but needing to set the boundaries.

"Do you think you'd be okay with that?"

Morena smiled ruefully. "It's been a long time since I've done something like that. Usually, it's more of a one-on-one, or three-some type of thing."

"I'm okay with that too."

She gently slapped his chest. "Of course you are. All men are."

"Have you ever been with two men?"

"Yes." Morena's voice was clear. There were many things in her past that she regretted but none that she was embarrassed about. "More than a few times."

"Men that like to be with each other too?"

"Once or twice." She looked at him carefully. "Have you?"

"Once or twice." He paused, choosing his words. "I have a friend."

CHAPTER FOUR

Lorde

G RACIE CLUTCHED THE HANDS of Lorde and Elizabeth and swung, tucking up her legs so her feet wouldn't drag on the ground. Cara had run ahead, holding the huge stuffed Pikachu Lorde had won for her.

If anyone had asked him a year ago what a Pikachu was, he might have thought they were talking about a new breed of monkey rather than a character from a video game. Things had changed a lot for Lorde.

It had been less than six months since Elizabeth had left her husband, Alan, and moved in with him, but for Lorde, it seemed like they had always been there. He was in love with Elizabeth but maybe more so with her girls, Grace and Cara; hopelessly, devotedly in love with them. In the short time he'd had them in his life, Lorde's world already revolved around them.

The last-minute decision to visit the fall fair in nearby Wolfville had been Lorde's suggestion, one he had been particularly proud of. He'd lived within twenty minutes of Wolfville and had never been at the fair. Never wanted to, even as a child himself. The rickety amusement rides that left riders clutching their stomachs were as bad as the grease-laden attempts at burgers and fries. And the games along the concession stands were there for the sole purpose to rid wallets of money.

Lorde had lost track of how many times he'd refused to go to the fair with his friend Meredith, or even with Elizabeth, way back in their youth.

Throw in the love of a child and Lorde was a new man.

"Up, up!" Gracie urged. It didn't take another cry to have Lorde lifting the eight-year-old high into the air, her kicking legs threatening his manhood.

He would do anything for the smile to stay on her face.

The four of them had settled into family life in his rambling farmhouse. Solo nights in front of the television were a thing of the past since the girls had their routines and forced Lorde to stick with them. School drop-offs, dance classes, and weekend birthday parties were the new norm. The sounds of *Dora the Explorer* and countless Disney sing-alongs took over the former silence of the house. Bella, the dog, had no complaints and seemed to enjoy the extra treats, picking up after the girls' snacks.

Life was good for Lorde, leaving little for him to brood about.

"Michael." The smile on Lorde's face faltered as he glanced over to where Elizabeth gestured. They were leaving for the evening, heading towards the gates of the fairground. "Is that...?"

"Fu—" Lorde bit back the curse that rose up at the sight of the well-dressed man striding through the gates. "I believe it is."

"Daddy!" Cara's shriek of delight caused Gracie to rip her hand out of Lorde's and race ahead to greet her father.

Elizabeth sighed. "Why did he have to show up here tonight?"

Lorde couldn't think of an answer that didn't portray Alan as even more of a monster than he was and took Elizabeth's hand instead.

It was a measure of Elizabeth's strength and her love for her daughters that the girls had no idea of the abuse their mother had endured at the hands of their father. His only saving grace, Elizabeth had said, was that he loved the girls more than life itself and would never do anything to hurt them.

Lorde had tried for months to get Elizabeth to press charges against Alan, but she'd demurred again and again.

"The girls would suffer. It's such a small town; people would talk. I don't want them to have any part of it."

The girls were the only reason Lorde hadn't gone himself. There was nothing he could do to make up for what Elizabeth had gone through, but at least he could make sure nothing like that happened again. Alan must have been aware Lorde watched him with eagle eyes.

Lorde tightened his grip on Elizabeth's hand as they approached, knowing Alan still made her uneasy. A woman stood with Alan, and Lorde watched the girls being introduced to her.

"Who's that?" Elizabeth murmured.

"No idea." Studying the tall blonde, Lorde at first felt disgusted that such a pretty woman would allow herself to be caught up in Alan's fake charm, but then a seed of recognition began to grow.

"Well, hello!" Alan boomed the greeting as they stopped. "Funny meeting you here."

"Funny, indeed," Lorde muttered.

"It's good to see you both, especially since I wanted to introduce Beth to the girls."

Lorde felt Elizabeth stiffen beside him. Her name was Beth? Blonde, pretty and named Beth? Lorde felt pretty sure he knew the dread Elizabeth felt since he felt it too.

"Michael, Elizabeth, this is my new friend Beth," Alan continued.

At the sight of her smile, things started clicking into place for Lorde. A few years ago, there had been a Beth who had worked for Morena. The jeans and sweatshirt fogged his memory of the statuesque woman in the tight, black dress who had helped pour drinks and serve dinner at Morena's weekend retreats, as well as help entertain the guests.

Lorde wondered if Alan knew how many times Beth had seen the inside of the cabins in the woods surrounding the inn.

"It's nice to meet you both," Beth said. Instead of avoiding Lorde's gaze, she met it head-on, giving him a strange smile and a hint of a wink.

"Daddy, Daddy, come see!" Gracie cried, tugging at Alan's hand. Alan smiled apologetically at Beth and let himself be led away.

"It's nice to see them together," Beth offered. "He was so happy to see them here."

"He used to be happy to see me too."

Lorde's gaze swivelled to Elizabeth, surprised at the acid in her voice.

"Did Alan tell you how happy he used to be when he saw me?" Elizabeth demanded. "When I did something he didn't like or forgot to do one of my chores? He would get so happy that he used to push me into a closet. Or once he punched me in the arm. He'd never let the girls see, but they were in the house so I couldn't really do anything about fighting back. But I should have. And I should tell you to stay away from him so he doesn't do the same thing to you."

Lorde had to give Beth credit; the woman didn't bat an eye. Her only reaction was to glance over her shoulder. "Alan and the girls are coming back."

"Do you not understand what I said? It's bad enough that I let it happen, but I can't let you be as blind as I was."

"I'm not blind, Elizabeth." Beth gave her a wide, friendly smile. "Hey, would you say hi to Morena for me?"

Grace and Cara swarmed Elizabeth, talking of games and prizes and it was a few minutes before Elizabeth could get them to leave. She stalked ahead with a frown on her face, leaving Lorde to carry a whining Cara to the car.

"What did she mean by that?" Elizabeth asked as they were buckling the girls into the car.

"Couldn't tell you." But Lorde had liked the wink Beth had given him and made up his mind to ask Morena what she was up to.

Chapter Five

Gemma

G EMMA SERVED JASPER A breaded chicken breast, smothered in tomato sauce and cheese. Her cooking was tolerable at best, at least if she stuck to basic Canadian dishes or the odd Italian. Spaghetti was her go-to meal, but tonight she'd combined it with the chicken for a change.

Change was good.

"This looks nice," Jasper praised, pouring her a glass of wine.

Gemma loved their quiet dinners together. For so many years of their marriage, they'd eaten on the run; Jasper too busy with his rising financial career to stop for a proper meal, and Gemma too consumed with her website *History by the Map*. While she had been working on her masters' degree in French history, she'd come up with the idea for an online site that showed a march through history with a series of changing maps. Using her artistic skills and memory for details, she'd grown the website into a teaching aid.

Her idea had paid off last year when she'd sold the site for a cool million dollars.

Now they had more than enough in the bank for romantic dinners out, but Gemma liked being home with Jasper.

She liked their life together.

"Are you all packed for this weekend?" Jasper asked as he helped her clear the table after they'd finished. "I think it's a great idea that we go a few days early. The bed and breakfast you found sounds perfect."

Gemma kept her head down and eyes averted. After a long day of deliberation after their book club meeting, she took Callie's suggestion and booked a weekend at Mrs. Robinson's before Jasper's conference began. They were leaving the day after tomorrow.

She hadn't told him everything about the inn.

She told herself that he'd be fine with it; be surprised but happy to try something new. But some part of her kept doubting the decision. Would he think he wasn't enough for her, that she needed something extra in their marriage?

Did she? If not, why the sudden desire to have sex with other people?

Gemma didn't know the answers and had stopped trying to figure it out. She only knew that she was excited about the thought.

Since the book club meeting earlier in the week, Gemma had read everything she could about swingers, including a couple of very R-rated novels.

She still got excited when she thought of what she had read and wondered if she might suggest the book club read them.

Gemma cleaned the counter while Jasper did the table, the two of them working well together like they always had. Six years of marriage and they were still compatible.

She was rinsing the dishcloth when Jasper's hand slid onto her backside.

"I like these pants. Are they new?"

"I've had them for a while."

He didn't reply as his hands roamed over her curves. Gemma liked her body, liked she had curves and an ass, and a fine set of breasts, according to Jasper. She liked that her husband still found her attractive.

Still wanted her.

Jasper stood behind her close enough that Gemma only needed to lean back slightly to touch him. Close enough to hear his breathing, feel his breath on the back of her neck. His hands slid down her legs, and she felt their warmth through the thin yoga pants she wore.

"I have basketball tonight," Jasper said in a low voice.

"I know."

"You'll be asleep before I get home."

"Probably." She paused as he pushed aside her hair, his lips brushing the side of her neck.

Just where she liked to be kissed.

"Unless you want me to wait for you," she said hopefully.

"You need your sleep."

She winced with disappointment, the grimace replaced by a smile as Jasper slid his hands up and under her thick sweater to cup her breasts.

Sex was no longer daily in the house, but it came pretty close.

Gemma leaned back against Jasper's chest as he cupped her breasts, toyed with her nipples. The world viewed her husband as quiet, serious and smart, well-spoken, cool and calm.

She knew a different side of him.

Gemma sucked in her stomach as one of his hands slid down, down, right under the waistband of her pants. Sucked in her breath as those wandering fingers met up with the elastic of her panties, and kept moving down.

She closed her eyes as he cupped her.

"Is this okay?" he whispered.

Gemma made a noise that was part moan, part chuckle. "You don't have to ask."

"I want you to ask."

The whimper escaped at his words. Each night was something different; Gemma was in awe of Jasper's creativity. Some nights he was rough, the next, so gentle Gemma would demand more. One night he tied her up and kept her on the verge of an orgasm for what seemed like hours; another night he took her without any consideration for her needs.

"Please."

"Please what?"

"Touch me. Make me come."

His fingers moved, finding her ready and willing. "Do you like it when I make you come?"

"I do..." She trailed off with a gasp as his finger found the sharp nub sending a burst of sensation through her.

"I like to hear you."

There was no way Gemma could be quiet as Jasper stroked and strummed her, meeting her needs an instant before she realized them. Her husband was very generous, she knew, reaching back to clutch a fistful of khakis as her head lolled back against his chest. He knew what she liked and what she didn't, what she was willing to try and what was beyond her comfort zone.

And he could make her come quicker than she could herself. Plus, he enjoyed doing it.

Gemma knew Jasper was smiling as he frantically rubbed her nub, enjoying her cries and moans as she fought to reach the edge. And then with a simple flick, he pushed her over, holding her upright as she shuddered to a close.

Without another word, Jasper had her pants down in a few quick moves. He pushed her head towards the counter, hiked her hips back against him. Jasper could be fast when he wanted, but he also knew when to take his time.

Tonight Gemma was in for a quickie.

She groaned as he slid into her, feeling the stretch, feeling the length of him. Closed her eyes as he began thrusting inside her.

Gemma loved being married to Jasper for many reasons but none seemed as important right now as the feel of him inside of her.

She clutched the counter as he took her harder, pulling out until just a tip was left, before slamming back inside. His hands held her hips tight as he thrust, again and again, and again.

"Oh…" The whimper became a moan, turned into a full-blown cry as he thrust harder, faster. She was back at the edge again, ready to tumble over again, when he suddenly stopped.

"No!" she cried as he pulled out. Then hands turned her, lifted her up.

"We haven't tried the counter in a while," Jasper said with a grin.

Gemma huffed a laugh as she took him in again, the granite cool under her backside. He held her legs and thrust inside as she fought to keep her balance. But the change wasn't enough of a distraction to keep her from getting closer and closer.

With a quick move of his hand, Jasper reached down to rub her clit. It was all Gemma needed to fall over the edge once more. And with a cry, Jasper joined her.

She held him against her until his breathing slowed, until she felt steady enough to stand.

"Have fun at basketball," she whispered.

CHAPTER SIX

Morena

DESPITE JED'S ATTEMPTS AT persuasion, Morena didn't stay the night with him. She left by midnight, making the quick and quiet drive back to the inn.

Living together would solve the problem of leaving a warm bed to make the cold drive home, but there were too many reasons not to make the jump.

Even though Morena wouldn't admit it to Jed, his age was top of her list.

As a fiftysomething woman, Morena was beyond proud she could still attract a man like Jed. Good-looking, decent, great in bed...

But deep down, the niggling fear wouldn't quiet. That Jed was only with her for a bit of fun. An adventure to put on his bucket list. He'd made no concessions about how he was adventurous and always looking for fun. A relationship with an older woman, especially one with her past, would be quite the coup.

She did her best to tell those fears to shut up but hadn't been successful yet. And she knew they were the reason she hadn't told Jed that she loved him. Jed was interested in her past, not intimidated by it. She'd never met a man who hadn't felt threatened by her in some way.

William hadn't been threatened by her, but that was because he wanted to possess her, body and soul.

Morena had eventually learned that about William Burgess, but that still didn't make it easier to get him out of her thoughts.

And she'd been thinking about him more and more lately. Maybe it was because things were so good with Jed. They were in sync with everything, on the same wavelength, despite their age. The age difference was Morena's only concern.

That, and Jed's request that his friend join them on the weekend.

She hadn't expected that.

But it wasn't a concern, just a surprise. Even though it shouldn't be. Jed may not have the colourful a history as Morena's, but he'd been part of the swinger lifestyle for most of his adult life. It was one of the things that had brought them together.

No, there was nothing wrong with her relationship with Jed. But despite this and the time they spent together, Morena still held back.

She'd never told him she loved him. Never examined herself to see if she did. Every time Morena had taken out the question, poised to find out what she truly thought about Jed, the thought of William loomed over her. Not only William but the memories of her husbands.

She'd made many mistakes with the men she'd cared about. Men she loved. She didn't want to do the same thing with Jed.

Now Thursday morning before a busy weekend, Morena had a list of things to finish before the guests began to arrive the next day. She also wanted a chance to think about what Jed had suggested.

Baking always helped clear her head. Morena checked the bread dough that she'd left out to rise, kneaded it and left it again before mixing a batch of cinnamon raisin cookies and one of chocolate chip.

Morena had an ache in her back before she'd even started on the batter for the muffins. She'd been running the inn for almost twenty years now, and each year she received a new ache or pain for her troubles. But she did it for the love of Fallen Gardens, of pride in her property because she certainly wasn't making that much money from running the B & B. It was too far out of town to get the tourist traffic. Unless people knew about it from word of mouth, her little place by the river was easily overlooked.

The swinger weekends were the only thing keeping her afloat these days.

Which was ironic, Morena thought as she measured batter into the muffin tins. Her past helped make her business a success, whereas when she had bought the tired old inn, she had been married to Bram, who had preferred to pretend his wife was as pure as the driven snow.

She always thought that was the reason Bram had run off with Lorde's mother. Bram hated knowing she'd been with other men; he'd accepted that she'd been married twice before, but refused to acknowledge or accept she'd been part of the swinger community.

She wondered if Bram would read the book Henry had written about her, chronicling her life and loves.

Henry, the son of friends, had grown up on the fringes of the community his parents belonged to. He knew all about swingers and other alternate lifestyles and wanted to write a book about it. He picked Morena as the focus of his book, and Morena surprised everyone when she agreed to the idea.

Morena had found talking about her past had been difficult at first, but the more she grew comfortable with Henry, the easier it became. When they reached the end of her story, leaving out her relationship with Jed, Morena found it cathartic and inspired her to think about the future.

She also grew quite close to Henry, even inviting him to live in one of the cabins where he had stayed while writing the book. He stayed at Fallen Gardens, living there with Iliya.

Both Henry and Morena had made the choice to leave Iliya out of the book, even with the numerous connections she had with Morena. None had been as significant as Iliya's life-changing relationship with William Burgess. Iliya and William's involvement had mirrored Morena—younger woman, older man looking to possess and dominate. To control.

After she had met Henry, Iliya had been able to put William behind her, a difficult achievement, as Morena well knew.

It had been over thirty years since she met William, but the man still kept tendrils entwined in Morena's life. She was sure it was the same with Iliya, but the younger woman seemed well-equipped to deal with the control-hungry William.

Morena wondered if it was time to tell William the book would be released soon.

Then she thought better of it. William Burgess was a private man, content to reign supreme over his sphere of influence, without letting the rest of society know about his proclivities. He would hate knowing there was a book published where he was mentioned, even though Morena had refused to use names. Such was William's vanity that he would assume readers would instantly know it was him who was being referenced.

There was no doubt William would be ready for a fight whenever he discovered a book about Morena was out there. Morena needed to be ready as well.

But not today. Today she had enough work to do to get ready for the guests to arrive. Almost a full house as well. It had been a while since Morena had so many reservations. She almost felt giddy with relief.

It was easier to focus on the relief rather than the extra workload of more people.

Morena started preparing more batter.

Morena was still deep in thought as she pulled a tray of muffins from the oven when the kitchen door swung open.

"Iliya." Morena only spared her a quick glance before turning to set the muffins on the cooling mat. Then she looked up again, this time catching Iliya's pale face and staring eyes. "What's happened?"

"It's William," Iliya whispered.

Morena frowned. William Burgess was her past, kept there by sheer willpower and knowing Iliya shared a similar history. Especially now they were friends. Friendly. Morena knew Iliya wasn't one for making friends, but she was sticking it out, for Henry's sake as well as her own. "Is he trying to make you come back to him?"

"He's dead!"

Time paused for Morena, slipped sideways. Suddenly it was months ago, and she was in the kitchen cleaning up after dinner. William had been there with Iliya for the weekend but had come to see her with an ulterior motive.

He always had a motive.

"Don't you love Iliya?" Morena had persisted. William had wanted her back, even with another woman in his life, in his bed. "Does she mean anything to you?"

"Not as much as you did," William muttered, slowing his on-slaught. "No one has ever been you."

It was the absolute vulnerability in his voice that had done it. Allowed Morena to reach out for him, to press her mouth against his, be swept back to the past.

That weekend had been the last weekend she'd seen him. And although the temptation had been strong, she'd said goodbye to him at the door.

"Dead?" Was that her voice? So distant and calm.

"Richard just texted me. They *texted* me to say he's dead. William–" Iliya's face crumpled and Morena pulled her into her arms.

Richard had the courtesy to call Morena but had to resort to leaving a message when Morena refused to answer. If she didn't hear the news from him, maybe it wasn't true. She could disregard

Iliya's emotions, but if Richard, William's lawyer and friend, told her the news...

It was hours later that Morena finally took a phone call. "Tia," she said in greeting when she recognized the number on the phone.

"Have you heard?" It had been Tia whom Morena ran to after her breakup with William, all those years ago. It was Tia who had always been there for her.

Morena closed her eyes, breathed deep. "How did it happen?"

"In his house. A heart attack. Funny–how many times did I suggest that he lacked a heart?"

Morena inhaled sharply at both the inappropriateness of the comment as well as the anger in Tia's voice.

But she didn't respond, only sat down on the edge of her little desk in the kitchen. Her to-do list was almost finished; most of the baking she liked to do for the guests was complete, and the only thing left to do was to go through the rooms one last time to make sure they were perfect for the guests. "He was here a few months ago."

Now it was Tia who inhaled sharply. "I didn't know that."

"Iliya's here. Do you know her? Of course you do."

"Morena, our circles are small and overlap a great deal. So that's where she went. I heard she just disappeared. It must have driven William crazy."

"She was here with him when she met Henry." Morena doodled on a pad of paper, never-ending circles, and spirals. She'd sent Iliya back to Henry earlier, hoping he would be able to comfort Iliya more than she could.

Morena couldn't be trusted to provide comfort to anyone until she figured out what she was feeling. Right now she was numb like her emotions had been wiped away with an eraser.

"Ah, Henry." Morena pictured Tia nodding her sleek head. "An odd couple but it could work."

"They seem to be happy together." And because she was thinking about love, Morena began drawing hearts entwined.

"How are you, Morena?" Tia's voice lost its anger, became gentle and caring as usual. "William was–"

"Part of my past," Morena interrupted in a firm voice.

"Yes, but an important part."

"But still, the past. He wanted more and I said no. I said–" Where had the tears come from? And the lump in her throat. William was her past.

"Morena?"

She fluttered her hand, sniffed quickly. "I'm fine. It's just a shock."

"Come to me. You shouldn't be alone."

Morena thought of the guests arriving tomorrow. "I won't be alone."

"Do you have people staying there? Are you having a weekend?"

"Check-in is four o'clock."

"I'm coming to you. No, don't argue–" Tia said over Morena's attempted protests. "You know I've been wanting to come for a visit for a while. This is the perfect time. I'll come for the weekend."

"I don't need help," Morena said feebly. "I have Lorde and Henry's here...Iliya..."

"Who won't be any help at all. Don't even try to argue. I'm online with the airline now." Morena could hear the click of the keyboard in the background. "There's a flight that gets in at noon. I'll be on that."

"Tia, thank you," Morena said in a rush, feeling her shoulder sag with relief. She didn't need help but the thought of a visit with Tia helped raise her spirits more than anything could.

CHAPTER SEVEN

Lorde

LORDE STROLLED THROUGH THE kitchen, his usual greeting hushed by the sight of Morena on the phone. He snagged a freshly baked cookie and headed for the lobby to stock the bar. Even though his participation in Morena's weekends had diminished with Elizabeth's arrival, he still continued to help out as much as he ever did.

He just didn't sleep with the guests any longer.

It had been the perfect solution while Elizabeth had been married to Alan. She had had Lorde's heart clutched firmly in her hand, so there had been no point in trying to meet anyone. He'd gone on a grand total of three dates in the years she had been married, each one more disastrous than the last.

Relationships were out of the question for Lorde, but a man had needs.

Morena's weekends were the perfect solution. An inn full of eager and excited women ready to experiment with a new partner, no strings attached. Most men would have thought they'd died and gone to heaven in that situation.

Lorde had enjoyed those years, enjoyed the women, but nothing could compare to the life he shared with Elizabeth now.

He was stocking the bar fridge with a bottle of champagne and wine when he noticed Morena at the kitchen door.

He was at her side in an instant. "What's the matter?"

She sighed deeply, her eyes red-rimmed like she'd been crying. Morena never cried. "I've had a bit of bad news."

He stared at her as she walked past him to the bar. It wasn't like Morena to show emotion, or be dramatic. He could picture little Cara flouncing past him refusing to answer him, but not Morena.

"What is it?" he demanded as she pulled a bottle of Scotch from the bar.

"William passed away."

He was at a loss for only a moment. "William–*William*, William?"

"Yes, the bane of my existence," Morena said with a humourless chuckle, splashing a healthy pour of spirit into a glass. "You know, I was just thinking about him while I was doing the baking, wondering if I should tell him that the book was coming out. Then I thought–no, I wouldn't, because I knew he'd be angry. Furious, and I wasn't in the mood for a fight. I guess I don't have to tell him now." She drank deeply, and Lorde, who had never learned to appreciate the burn of a good Scotch, winced at the speed she emptied the glass.

"What happened?"

Morena poured herself two more fingers. "Heart attack. Yes, apparently, he did have a heart. It was the first thing Tia said. That's who I was talking to. She'll be here tomorrow. I'm sure she'd be on a flight right now if she could find one."

"That's good." What else could he say? Lorde wasn't an emotional man. Sometimes he wondered if that was what drew him to Morena. They were friends, more like mother and son, and more alike than most people realized. He knew Morena would talk if she wanted to talk, and if so, he'd be there for her.

"It will be good to see her."

He'd met Tia only a few times, but the way Morena talked about her friend made Lorde feel like he knew her.

"Tia's always good to have in a crisis," Morena said, already halfway through her second drink. "Not that this is a crisis. I've lost track of the times I've run to her in times of trouble. Or heartbreak. If I didn't have an almost full house, I'm sure I'd be running to her this time too. That reminds me, I should check to make sure I have room for her. Wouldn't that be horrible if I didn't?"

"She could stay with me."

She met his gaze, acknowledging his offer without saying a word. Letting him know she appreciated him being there for her. She rifled through her reservations ledger. Lorde found it strange for a woman with all the latest technologies, Morena preferred to go old-school with her reservations. She had a website for people to book rooms, but when they arrived, she signed them in using pen and paper.

Lorde liked that about her.

"Two rooms left. Can you believe it? Almost a full house. I don't know how long it's been since we've had that many here for a weekend."

"I've got the cabins ready."

"Thank you, Michael. You'll be at dinner? You and Elizabeth? I know what you've decided." She paused, not wanting to discuss something so intimate with him. "But I like having you here."

"I'll be here. Do you need anything else?" He didn't know what to say about her evident grief. Elizabeth would be better equipped to deal with this. Women were better with emotional things.

Anyone was better at it than he was.

"I'm not sure what I would need." Morena lifted her shoulders limply. "He was part of my past, but that's all. I'm not sure what I should be feeling."

"You should feel grief and sadness. Regret that your last meeting with him wasn't as you'd hoped. No matter how you left it with him, I'm sure you'll feel regret about something."

"I do," she admitted, swirling the liquid in the glass.

"You can feel anger and remorse. And maybe even a bit of relief."

"I feel all those things."

"I think that's normal."

"Then I'm behaving normally? Even though I want nothing more than to drink enough of this Scotch to be able to blot out everything I may be feeling? Whenever I start to feel something, that is. Right now I'm numb."

"Again, that's normal."

"Normal," she scoffed, draining her glass. Lorde picked up the bottle and poured a refill, hesitating a moment before he added the last finger. "Normal was the last thing William was. I can't even call him a good man. He was generous when he wanted to be, but he could be cruel. Even in..."

Lorde knew she was referring to William's proclivities in the bedroom and glad she didn't elaborate.

"William needed to control his environment, and that meant every person in it. For years, I didn't realize what he was doing but when I did, I thought I could change him." Morena heaved a sigh. "I thought I could make him a better man."

"You couldn't," Lorde said, his tone blunt and no-nonsense.

"No, I couldn't." She sighed sadly. "No one can change a person if they don't want to be changed. I wasted many years thinking I could. Too many years."

"It wasn't a waste."

"How can you say that? You have no idea about the relationship between us. Some days I wonder if I knew anything about it, and I was part of it. William was...complex. Confusing. An asshole at times."

"Maybe so, but being with him made him you who you are. Everything in your past has helped make you the person you are today. If you didn't survive William, who knows if you would have been strong enough to get through Bram leaving, and creating this." Lorde waved his hands to encompass the lobby. "He made you who you are–the good and the bad."

Morena stared into her glass, the smell of Scotch wafting up Lorde's nose. He disliked the smell of it, but still, he stood there with her.

After a few moments of the tableau, Morena looked up as if surprised to see him still there. "You can do what you need to do, Michael. I'm fine."

"I know, but I want to make sure."

She smiled fondly. "You're very good to me, you know."

His heart shifted in his chest, the same feeling he always got whenever they let their guard down. "I think it goes both ways."

At her nod, Lorde drew a deep breath. "There's something else I wanted to ask you about. We saw Beth the other night."

Morena's expression transformed from melancholy to guarded happiness. "How is Beth?"

"Beth is with Alan. But you knew that, didn't you?" Morena swirled the last of her Scotch instead of answering. "What did you do?"

"Nothing. Yet."

"Morena, you know what Alan is like. What he did to Elizabeth."

"Michael, you know I adore Elizabeth. But the only thing I can't comprehend is how she let him get away with treating her like that. I know she won't press charges in case the girls are caught in the crossfire, but there has to be some way. And then I wondered what would happen if he tried that on someone else?"

"So you set up Beth to date him? Why would you do that? He'll hurt her." At the thought of Beth at the mercy of Alan, Lorde's frustration had him balling his fists.

Morena gave a tinkle of laughter. "Beth can more than take care of herself. Do you know that she has a black belt in karate? As well as having taught her own self-defence class? I told her about Alan and Elizabeth, and I think she wants Alan to try something like that as much as I do."

Lorde stared at her, wanting to argue, to demand Morena stop this insane plan, but part of him marvelled at Morena's deviousness.

"Just leave it be, Michael," Morena said in a quiet voice. "No harm will come to Beth."

"You can't be sure." He worried about Beth, but if she was that capable, it might be worth it to see Alan get his comeuppance. "How can she stand to be with him?"

This time Morena laughed loudly. "That's the best part. Beth was also an actress in Charlottetown. You honestly didn't think I was about to let that man get away with trying to get me arrested, did you? As well as what he put poor Elizabeth through?"

Lorde gave her a grudging smile. "You're a bit of a badass, aren't you?"

Morena patted his hand. "You've no idea."

CHAPTER EIGHT

Gemma

A S THEY STEPPED OFF the plane in Halifax, Gemma was filled with a mixture of excitement and foreboding. They had arrived early for Jasper's conference and were renting a car to drive to the little town of Wolfville on the edge of the Bay of Fundy where Mrs. Robinson's Bed and Breakfast was located.

Gemma still hadn't told Jasper about the swingers. That they were going to spend their romantic weekend away with other couples who liked to swap partners.

She had no idea what she was going to do. How to tell him, and when she did–because he really deserved to know–how to react to his reaction? Whether it be anger and disappointment, an insistence to leave, or if he was happy and excited that she had booked the weekend for them.

Gemma honestly didn't know what would be worse.

She'd never kept anything from Jasper, not even the time she ran into the pillar in the underground parking lot and dented his car. It would have been so easy to blame it on an unknown person doing a dent and dash, but Gemma was an honest person. She valued honesty and communication in her marriage.

So why didn't she tell Jasper she wanted to have sex with another man tonight?

"Wow," Jasper said as they got their first glance at the inn.

"It's beautiful," she agreed, drinking in the sight of the three-story, century-stone farmhouse set high on a hill. Wings stretched wide on either side of the double doors, with a wide, covered porch running the length. A copse of trees circled the inn with a hint of water in the distance.

Jasper reached over and squeezed her hand. "This was a good idea. We can head to Halifax Sunday for the conference, but it'll be nice to have a couple of days just us together."

This was the perfect time to confess, to admit what she had planned.

"Together," Gemma echoed, her voice sounding a little strained in her ears. Maybe they could be together–have sex with strangers together. Gemma had no idea how things would work. *If* they would even work. Jasper might well turn the car around when he found out.

It was a delicate balance telling your husband that you wanted to bring someone else into the marriage.

Darn Callie for suggesting this. Or maybe, yay for Callie.

Gemma had no idea what was about to happen in the next five minutes. They were here.

Jasper parked the car, turned to her with a grin. "Let's go check in."

"Jasper…" He paused with the car door already open, looking every inch like a man raring to get in and find another sex partner. Gemma shook her head. "Never mind. This will be fun."

She carried one of her bags, while Jasper took the other one along with his suitcase, briefcase, and laptop. Trailing after him, Gemma tried to still her knocking knees as they climbed the steps onto the porch. Colourful Muskoka chairs were set in conversation areas against the side of the inn, each grouping set up with wool blankets and a portable fireplace to keep out the chill.

Huge double wooden doors led into the lobby. Inside, wood-panelled walls, dark hardwood floors, and bursts of colour provided by chairs and couches scattered throughout the space. Abstract pictures hung on the walls.

A roaring fire completed the picture, along with the giant Christmas tree standing in the centre of the lobby as if waiting to be decorated.

To the right of the double doors was a bar set into the brick wall, complete with rustic wooden beams, leather padded stools, and shelves holding bottles of every shape and size and variety.

"Welcome to Fallen Gardens," the woman behind the bar said with a welcoming smile. Her long white hair and perfectly etched lines on her face only improved her features, transforming her from an attractive older woman to a stunning one. "I'm Morena."

Gemma felt both intimidated and caught up in the thrall of a powerful girl crush as they walked towards the bar.

"I thought it was called Mrs. Robinson's?" Jasper asked, setting his bags down. His gaze roamed the lobby, taking in everything, but it wasn't until he turned back to Morena that his eyes widened with appreciation.

"The property was named Fallen Gardens when I bought it, oh, quite some time ago. But everyone thinks of me as a bit of a Mrs. Robinson, so that's what it's called."

Gemma's mouth was as dry as a desert. "The Mrs. Robinson from the movie? The one with the younger man?"

What on earth was she thinking of bringing them here? This was completely out of their league.

"That's the one." Morena smiled knowingly at them. Gemma wondered if this would be when Jasper called foul, but he was looking at Morena with as much interest in his eyes as Gemma was. "But to tell you the truth, age isn't really a big factor for me."

"That's good," Gemma said for lack of anything else. "It's nice to be inclusive." She stared around the lobby with terror in her heart as Jasper checked them in, waiting for the moment that Morena asked them about their history as swingers. Did they prefer a full swap, or just to add a partner? Were they supposed to book an extra room or use the one they were sharing?

"What brings you here?" Morena asked. As the paperwork was finished, she pulled out a pitcher and a bottle from the fridge. Gemma watched Morena partially fill two glasses with the pink liquid before she expertly uncorked the sparkling wine and topped up the glasses.

She desperately needed a drink because as soon as they went upstairs, she was going to have to tell Jasper what was really going on in this place.

"I have a conference in Halifax next week," Jasper explained. "We thought a weekend away beforehand would be nice."

"Perfect. A little fun before you get down to work." She pushed the glasses before them.

Jasper glanced down at Gemma. "Something like that."

Gemma took a welcome suck from the straw. Tart sweetness exploded on her tongue. "What is this?" she asked, more to change the subject than real curiosity.

"Cranberry cosmopolitan with a splash of prosecco to make it bubbly. I thought it was a nice lead-up for the holidays. I'm putting everyone to work tomorrow." She motioned to the tree looming over the lobby. "Tree-trimming party."

"Sounds perfect," Jasper said with a smile. "And there's a dinner tonight?"

"Our sit-down dinner, yes. It'll be a little more formal than tomorrow night. And we've got a full house this weekend so there will be plenty of others to keep you interested. A few first-timers like yourself, but there's plenty of couples who have been here before who will be happy to show you the ropes."

There it was. Gemma held her breath and readied for the outburst.

"What kinds of ropes?" Jasper asked, in his matter-of-fact way.

"Well, you can find silk scarves in every cabin and I think there might be some cable ties–"

"Maybe we'll just head up to our room," Gemma interrupted, clutching Jasper's arm.

"Of course. Let me just give you a key." Morena looked up as the front door opened, her face softening into an expression of such happiness that Gemma felt her own heart twist with joy. "Tia. And, oh–Jacey and Dominic." Without another word to Gemma and Jasper, Morena rushed out from behind the bar to hurry toward the door.

Gemma watched as the four exchanged heartfelt hugs.

"Should we wait?" Jasper whispered.

"We don't have a key," she hissed. So close–she was so close.

"I'm sorry. That was rude," Morena called, returning to the bar with the threesome in tow. "It's just that these are my very dear friends who I haven't seen in so long. Gemma and Jasper, this is Tia, Dominic, and Jacey."

"Jacey and Jasper? I think we need to do something with that." The tall woman with the riot of curls gave a belly laugh. Gemma didn't know where to look first–Jacey's hair or her piercing eyes, or the chest with enough cleavage flashing to drown a small child.

"Definitely." Jasper gave a hearty chuckle and Gemma gasped. Did Jasper just finagle an assignation with the woman? Just like that?

"Maybe we could meet in the hot tub after we check in?" Jacey suggested, prompting a grin from Dominic.

"You don't waste any time, do you?"

Jacey rolled her eyes. "What's the point in that?"

CHAPTER NINE

Morena

Morena watched as Jasper and Gemma climbed the stairs. "I don't think he has any idea what he's in for this weekend."

"Isn't that the fun of it?" Jacey asked, twining her arm through Tia's. "He's cute. I was completely serious about the hot tub. Ever since Wendy and Jackson put one in, I can't get enough of the things."

Morena smiled at the younger woman, still as forthcoming and honest as ever. "It's so good to see you, Jacey. Both of you. All of you." She felt the prickle of tears in her eyes as she met Tia's gaze. "I'm so glad you came."

Tia reached out to squeeze her hand. "No place we'd rather be."

"When Tia told us her plans, we thought that was a perfect opportunity for another visit," Dominic said. "Sort of like a chaperone."

"Like that's the last thing Tia needs," Jacey scoffed. "She's a grown woman. Tough as nails."

"Why, Jacey, I never knew you cared," Tia teased and smiled and Jacey's cheeks flushed a pretty pink.

Morena had gotten to know Jacey and Dominic during their first visit to the inn and had kept in touch with the couple since then. She knew Tia was quite fond of both of them and didn't feel slighted they had joined her for the trip.

Dominic touched her arm. "We were so sorry to hear about your friend."

"Thank you," Morena said automatically.

"That's why I let him deal with the important, personal stuff," Jacey announced, reaching for three glasses on the bar and filling them with the cranberry cosmopolitan mix. Morena topped them with Prosecco. "I don't get what you're supposed to say when someone dies. I never could understand it. I would end up saying something like "Oops, he's dead.""

Morena blanched as Dominic rolled his eyes and Tia chuckled. They were well aware of Jacey's idiosyncrasies. And Morena knew Jacey didn't mean any harm, but the word *dead* rang in her ears.

Dead dead dead.

"Were you very close to him? Is that better?" Jacey asked apologetically as if she sensed Morena's distress. For someone who often missed obvious social cues, Jacey was very perceptive about a person's emotions.

"He was a big part of my past," Morena said firmly, hoping to change the subject.

"Who else do we have joining us this weekend?" Tia asked, her eyes searching Morena's face, who smiled sadly, letting her know that she was okay.

Of course she was okay. William was her history, nothing more. She had made that perfectly clear the last time she saw him.

Morena pulled her reservation book across the counter. It was old school, but she liked seeing the list of names every weekend. The book was also kept in her safe in her main office. As Henry pointed out when he was writing her memoirs, those lists of names could be worth a whole lot of money if it fell into the wrong hands.

The swinger community was tight-knit, but far-reaching and contained several surprises that the general population would find more than interesting.

"The fab foursome is back again," Morena said to Tia. She and Tia had been close to Brian, Liliane, Richard, and Heidi in their youth. "They were booked even before we heard about William. Apparently, Richard is his power of attorney...was. He was his power of attorney, so we'll be able to find out more."

"What else do you need to know?" Jacey asked bluntly. "How he died?"

"Jacey," Dominic hissed.

Morena stared at Jacey. She knew Jacey, knew her quirks and wasn't offended. It was a good question, for what else *did* Morena need to know about the death of a man from her past.

"If he was alone," she finally replied. "I hope there was someone with him."

Jacey opened her mouth to speak, but Dominic elbowed his wife. The move brought a smile to Morena's face. She could only imagine what Jacey was about to say.

She continued to read off a few names from her list with Tia nodding acknowledgement of a few.

Tia had a finger in everyone's pie.

"And Lorde?" Jacey asked, eagerly enough for Dominic to cock an eyebrow in her direction.

"He may join us for dinner," Morena explained. "But that would be it. He keeps Elizabeth fairly close."

"I'm glad it worked out for him," Jacey said. Another eyebrow from Dominic. "What? I am! He's a nice guy. I want him to be happy."

"And you're not a little bit disappointed that he won't be happy in your bed?" Dominic chided.

Jacey's reaction was to throw her arms around her husband. "Will you listen to him? How weird is it that my husband is teasing me about another man?"

"And I'm glad this lifestyle has worked out for you." Morena smiled. "But I don't think Michael is quite there yet. Elizabeth is very precious to him. But there is someone for you to meet. My friend, Jed."

Jacey's jaw dropped. "Seriously? You want me with your guy?"

"Jed's friend will be staying with us," Morena finished with a wide smile. "I haven't met him yet. You'll have to give me your impressions."

"You and Jed and the friend?" Jacey asked with an approving gleam in her eyes.

"I didn't–I don't–" Morena stammered.

"Two guys and one girl," Jacey marvelled. She turned to Tia. "I used to want to be like you when I grew up, but after hearing about this, now I'm not sure. I think it's a tie between the both of you."

"And with that, I think we'll head up to our room," Dominic said. He took a protesting Jacey by the arm, appeased only by a bottle of champagne and promises to meet in the hot tub shortly.

Morena watched the couple head up the stairs. "She hasn't changed."

"I think she might be getting more sociable with the others," Tia admitted. "They seem to be rubbing off some of her rough edges. But of course, I wonder if that's really a good thing."

Morena laughed. "Jacey is a wonder, and Dominic has the patience of a saint."

"Thank goodness he doesn't live as one." Tia winked at Morena, before sliding around the counter to engulf her in a hug.

Morena relaxed in her embrace, never realizing how much she needed a friend until Tia was here.

"How are you?" Tia demanded in a gentle voice.

"Oh, I don't know. I'm fine–really. But I can't get my head around that William's gone. It's such a shock. And, well, the way I left things with him. It feels unfinished somehow."

"You weren't going to take him back, Morena, so stop thinking like that. He suggested; you refused. Politely, I'm sure, which was more than he deserved."

Morena pulled away at the harsh tones, unspoken questions on her lips.

"You're right. I did not like the man. I know it's wrong to speak ill of the dead, but Morena, watching what he did to you? To Iliya? You know I'm not one to judge people's proclivities, and I'm not. It's his behaviour outside the bedroom that I disliked. He was control hungry; he needed to possess everyone he was involved with."

"He was a Dom," Morena defended him.

Tia tapped her nails on the counter like she was searching for words. "I've known my share of Doms, and William was much more," she said finally. "He was a sadist, but there was a cruel streak to him in real life. That's what I never liked. I knew what he was like as a businessman, and I was so afraid he would take that ruthlessness to the bedroom. I didn't want you to be hurt."

"He never hurt me," Morena said, then paused. "Not like that. Not much."

"He would have tried to block the publication of your book. You know that, don't you?"

"Which is why things were so quiet. I asked for no advance publicity just in case. It's funny," she mused. "I had just been thinking that I should tell him before I got word. Things will be starting to heat up in about six weeks, but I kept putting off telling him. And now I don't have to."

"If William knew there was a book being published that would demonize him in any way, trust me, the man would have stuck around."

"You're probably right." She sighed.

"Of course I am. Now, on to bigger and better topics. When am I going to meet this man of yours?"

"At dinner." The smile was across her face before she realized it. It seemed impossible for her to smile moments after discussing William, but somehow even the faintest thought of Jed lightened her mood.

"Oh, Morena!" Tia clapped her hands with delight. "You're in love with him."

CHAPTER TEN

Lorde

LORDE LINGERED IN THE kitchen. He'd come to help Morena with the guests, any mundane task she wanted to give him to do. He didn't know any other way to help her with her grief.

Was she grieving? What had William been to her? Lorde knew they had once been close, but his relationship was such with Morena, that Lorde never asked details.

The thought made him squeamish, much like thinking of his mother being with another man.

Lorde wondered if that man was still Bram since they had run off together in the dead of night when Lorde had been seventeen.

But Lorde didn't want to think about Morena or his mother, or any other female right then.

Because as he peered through the tiny window in the door leading out to the lobby, he saw that Jacey was here.

Jacey was back, standing right by the bar, almost in the same place that she had been when he last saw her.

After they...

They what? Spent the night together? Made love? Had some of the best sex in Lorde's life?

And now she was standing right there, not ten feet away from him.

He waited, watched through the little window and felt like a stalker but couldn't bring himself to go and greet her. There was something about Jacey that had gotten under his skin.

And into his pants as well.

How could he think of another woman when he was so in love with Elizabeth? Lorde didn't want to remind himself that he'd been in love with Elizabeth when he'd slept with Jacey the first time.

As well as a variety of other women.

Lorde leaned his head against the door, desperately thinking of something, anything that would relieve the stiffness in his cock. Seeing Jacey made him remember what she felt like–the softness of her skin, the touch of her hands.

The sounds she made.

"Hey, man!"

Lorde whipped around at the sound of the voice. Jed grinned as he stepped into the kitchen, bringing in a gust of cold air as well as another man. "You okay?"

"Good," Lorde said as he stepped away from the door. "Just...thinking for a sec."

Jed glanced at him curiously. "It happens."

He glanced at the other man, tall and blond with movie-star good looks. Even Lorde, without any attraction to men, could admit this guy was something.

Not that Jed wasn't anything to write home about. Lorde liked Jed. He was a decent man and good to Morena. Of course, if he hadn't been, Jed wouldn't have lasted long. He admitted the age difference had been a little jarring at first, but Elizabeth had reminded him again and again that Morena's happiness was all that mattered.

"Listen," Jed toed off his boots and padded across the floor in vibrantly striped socks. "I want you to meet a friend of mine. Coulter, this is Lorde; Lorde, Coulter Wylde. I've known him since–how long has it been?"

"Too long," Coulter said with a good-natured grin. "Is that what the ladies call you?"

"If they want me to answer. Michael Lorde," Lorde conceded. "But no one calls me Michael."

"Except for his ladies," Jed said. "Elizabeth and Morena."

"Where is the lovely Elizabeth?" Jed asked, glancing towards the kitchen.

"Seeing the girls off. I'll bring her over for dinner later."

"Lorde's wife. But she's not your wife, is she? Seems like it, you playing house with her," Jed began.

"Hope to be soon enough." Lorde's guard was down; the only reason he let any mention of his dream slip out.

"Really?" Jed whistled. "That's cool. Make an honest woman out of her. And with a better man than last time."

Jed knew as much as Morena did about Elizabeth's marriage to Alan.

"Elizabeth is the prettiest little thing–just a sweetheart," Jed continued. "I love her to death."

Lorde hid his smile. He wondered if Jed's adoration of Elizabeth would change if he knew Elizabeth had woken him that morning with his cock in her mouth, demanding he fuck her. She might be a sweetheart, but she was a sexy one at that, with a mouth like a trucker when she wanted him.

Elizabeth wanted him. A smile slid over his face at the thought.

"You can see her at dinner," Lorde said to Coulter.

"And after dinner?" Coulter asked. "Isn't that the plan here? A nice dinner and even nicer dessert?"

Lorde's smile slid right off his face. "We go home after dinner."

"That's a shame," Coulter said lightly.

Lorde's face warmed. If he didn't know better...He noticed Jed's smirk. It had been several years since a man came on to him, but at least he still recognized it when it happened.

Coulter raised his eyebrow in a perfect Jack Nicholson impersonation. "So I thought Morena was *your* lady?" he asked Jed.

"Lorde's known her longer, since he was a wee little boy."

"Ah." Coulter gave a nod of his blond head. "Mother issues."

"There's no issues," Lorde said angrily.

"'Course not. Coulter's just pulling your chain. He does that." Jed slapped a hand across his friend's chest. "Stop it."

Coulter responded by sticking out his hand. "Mr. Lorde. It's a pleasure to meet you."

Lorde battled by handshake, squeezing tighter than Coulter.

"So who's out there?" Jed asked, taking Lorde's spot at the window.

"Tia and..." Lorde glanced out, relief pooling in his stomach. Jacey was gone, as well as Tia. "Tia. I was giving them time to talk before I burst in."

"Well, let's burst because my lady is all by her lonesome." Jed gave Coulter another backhand across the chest. I can't wait for her to meet you."

CHAPTER ELEVEN

Gemma

"THIS PLACE IS GREAT," Jasper said as he dropped their bags on the floor of their room. It was painted a silvery blue with a white dresser and desk, with a huge bed covered in a white quilt and mounds of pillows.

Gemma wished she could bury herself under the pile of pillows and not have this conversation. "Jasper, there's something I have to tell you."

"Look at the view," he marvelled. "You can see the Bay of Fundy from here."

She quickly glanced out the window, noticed the silver streak of water leading to the Atlantic Ocean. It was a pretty view, one she might have appreciated if her stomach hadn't been tied in knots. She sat down on the bed, tucking her cold hands between her knees. "Jasper, those people downstairs–"

"She was amazing looking," Jasper swung around to see her seated on the bed. "Not that you have to worry, because there's no way I'd have a chance, even if I wanted to." His brow furrowed. "Although it kind of seemed like she was flirting with me, as unbelievable as that sounds."

"What if you did have a chance with her?" Gemma asked weakly.

"Like that's going to happen." Jasper prowled into the bathroom. "This is great too. I'm so glad there's an ensuite because I hate when you have to go out into the hall to–"

"Jasper!" Gemma's voice was tinged with desperation, which made Jasper poke his head out of the washroom. "I'm trying to tell you something."

"About the woman downstairs. Because you know you don't have to worry about it, don't you? I love you, Gemma and only you."

"It's about the woman, but I'm not worried. Jasper, this place is for swingers. She is a swinger. They're all swingers–maybe together, maybe not, I don't know."

Jasper gave a bark of laughter. "Swingers? How would you know that?"

"Because this place is a resort for swingers. A swinger's resort. People come here to swing." Gemma heaved a sigh of relief that it was done but now was the hard part. Jasper's reaction.

"What do you mean, this is a swingers resort?" Jasper demanded. "Like a singles resort, but for swingers?"

"I think so."

"What exactly is a swinger?"

"A person who engages in group sex or swaps partners," Gemma recited. "At least that's what Wikipedia says."

"Group sex? Swapping? And you brought *us* here?" Jasper sat down heavily on the bed. "Gemma, what's going on?"

"I thought you'd like some excitement," she whispered.

"*Me*?"

"We've been married six years and you know what they say about the seven-year itch? I wanted to try and head it off, make you so happy that you wouldn't think of–" She was babbling, she knew she was babbling but she couldn't seem to stop.

"I am happy with you, Gemma. This is..." Jasper shook his head. "Are you serious?"

"Would you want to?" she asked desperately.

"Would *you*?"

"That woman...that Jacey downstairs...she was looking at you."

"Is that what she meant? Is that what she wanted?" Jasper had a stunned expression on his face, one that would have had Gemma bestowing kisses on his adorable face if the situation hadn't been so tense. "Really?"

"I think so. I don't really know. My friend Callie told me about this."

"Is she one of these swingers?"

"I don't really know. I don't know her all that well."

"Wow." He looked at her, searching for answers in her eyes. "Is this what you want, Gemma?"

"I don't know," she said quickly. "Maybe."

"Am I not enough for you?"

"Jasper, no. You're so giving and generous and sexy, and you've got the best cock–"

"Gemma..."

"No, really, you do. You're such an amazing lover and we've always had fun with trying new things. Remember when you tied me up with your tie, and then that time with the ice cube –"

"Gem*ma*!"

"I love you, Jasper, so much. But I thought this might be fun to try."

The words hung between them. Jasper reached up and pushed an errant curl behind Gemma's ear and sighed. "Fun to try."

"We don't have to if you don't want to. But...I've never been with anyone else."

"It's not like I'm a man of experience. I count *two* before you." Another sigh. "Maybe we should go find this hot tub."

"Really?"

He held up his hand. "I'm not promising anything. I can't, because I don't know what's going on. I'd like to talk to people, before... I'd need to talk to them."

Her heart was beating wildly. Was he serious? Were they really going to do this? "Of course. I don't think we jump in and start doing it."

"What exactly would we be doing?"

"I think that's up to us, and the others...other couple...other person."

"It could be us and someone else?"

"Another man, yes."

"Why not another woman?" Jasper asked quickly.

"I–uh, I guess...Whatever you want. I wouldn't know what to do, though."

"And you think I do?"

"I think you can handle yourself with another woman," Gemma assured him.

Jasper stared at her in disbelief before pulling her in for a hug. "I don't believe you."

"I'm sorry I didn't tell you."

"How is that even possible? You tell me every time you find a sale at Loblaws."

"It was really hard," Gemma said, her voice muffled by his shoulder. His strong, sexy shoulders that he was going to show to another woman. Gemma pulled back. "Are you sure about this?"

"I'll say it again. Are you?"

"We don't have to do anything. We can just go down and meet some people."

"I can meet people. I'm good at meeting people."

"You're very good at meeting people."

There was a pause as Gemma asked herself if this was what she wanted. Finally, Jasper exhaled in a huff. "Well, let's do this if we're going to. Do you think we wear bathing suits in the hot tub?"

CHAPTER TWELVE

Morena

MORENA WATCHED TIA CLIMB the stairs.

It was so good to see Tia. Morena was comfortable spending her free time with younger women like Elizabeth and Iliya, but it was nice having a friend her own age in the house.

And for Jacey and Dominic to join her.

"Did I miss her?"

Morena's smile widened as Jed walked in. Jed, and a blond, blue-eyed, very tall drink of water. Her eyes flicked back to him as the two approached followed by Lorde. "Tia? Yes, but she's looking forward to meeting you at dinner. Lorde, did you see who joined her? Jacey and Dominic are here as well."

"Are they now?"

"They came with Tia as a surprise. It's lucky I could still find them a room. It hasn't been this busy for a long time."

"Have many of your friends come because of him...William?" Jed asked.

"Just Tia, and now Jacey and Dominic. Brian and Liliane were already booked, but Richard and Heidi changed their plans to come."

"Morena lost a friend a few days ago," Jed explained to Coulter.

"If you could call him that," Lorde muttered under his breath as he headed for the fireplace to check the burning logs. Morena frowned after him, watching as he left out the door leading to the woodpile.

"Could this Tia be interested in meeting me as well?" the blond said, pulling her attention away from the brooding Lorde. "I'd love if my arrival made you that happy."

"I can't say if she'd be pleased," Morena replied, even though her internal thoughts were screaming yes. There would be many happy women at the table that night with him sitting across from them. "You'd have to ask her yourself."

"I might just have to do that." He smiled at her, a blinding white smile with the perfect teeth only years of orthodontist work could provide.

He had dimples, dimples deep enough to lose a finger in.

Jed cleared his throat, and Morena tore her gaze away from him with more than a twinge of guilt. "Are you about finished?"

"Not even started," he replied, giving her another toe-tingling smile.

Who was he?

"Morena, this is Coulter," Jed said, slapping a hand on his shoulder.

From a distance, the two could be brothers with tousled blond hair and blue eyes. But with a closer inspection, the differences were there. Jed's hair was tousled by the wind and his hands, while

Coulter's 'do looked as if it was produced by countless minutes by the mirror and several hair products.

It didn't make him any less good-looking.

Never before had Morena been conscious of how much Jed looked like a country boy. She loved that about him, appreciated the faded jeans that hugged his narrow hips, and the stomach flattened by years of manual labour. But Coulter, with his tapered pants and fine cotton shirt, was all city compared to Jed.

She took the hand Coulter offered, felt the strength, the faint calluses of his palms.

What would a hand like that feel like on her body?

She shocked herself with the thought. It had been a long time since Morena had been to church, but she had to admit Coulter had a face like an angel. "It's nice to meet you."

Coulter squeezed her hand, practically bowing over it. "I've heard so many things about you."

She glanced at Jed. "And I've heard...really nothing about you."

Coulter laughed, the sound as sexy as expected. "You win. Jed's always a bit close-mouthed and hasn't told me much either. Only that there is a woman, as sexy as hell. He said something about an age difference, but it's no more than a couple of years, is it?"

"Oh, you're good." She tried to pull her hand away but Coulter's grip was firm.

"I hope you'll be finding out just how good."

Another glance at Jed, who shrugged. "Coulter's a little direct."

"More like, when I see something I want, I go and get it. And you, mystery woman, I decided I wanted you as soon as I walked in here."

"Maybe you should meet the rest of the guests." Morena's gaze flickered again to Jed. Were they really doing this? Other than the quick mention the other night, they hadn't talked at all about it. Jed had tried last night, but Morena had been overwhelmed with the news of William's death and hadn't felt like talking about anything.

Jed slapped a hand on Coulter's shoulder. "We'll have a good night."

They were doing it.

She glanced at Coulter who grinned at her. She couldn't get over those dimples. And the mouth between them—full, sexy lips demanding to be kissed.

Jed was watching her with a hopeful expression on his face.

Two handsome men for her for the night? There were worse things.

CHAPTER THIRTEEN

Lorde

BY THE TIME LORDE returned with an armful of firewood, the lobby was deserted. He guessed that Morena had gone with Jed to show Coulter to his room.

He wondered what else she'd be showing him.

Lorde gave his head a shake. Where did that come from? Morena was a grown woman, capable of making her own decisions. Who she wanted to spend her time with, in whatever capacity, was no business of his.

He finished stacking the wood when the gust of cold air behind him announced the arrival of more guests.

"Well, aren't you a sight for sore eyes!"

Lorde straightened up in time for Liliane to come barrelling into him, throwing her arms around his waist.

"Hello to you too," he said awkwardly. The woman was practically squeezing the life out of him. He glanced over the top of her head. "Richard."

"Hello, Lorde." The older man glanced around the lobby. "No Morena?"

"Showing a guest to his room."

"Was he a cute one?" Liliane asked as she released him.

"Depends on your definition of cute."

"No one is as cute as you," she said, reaching up as if to pinch his cheeks. Lorde stepped quickly out of her reach.

"Leave the boy alone," Richard demanded in a good-natured voice, following Lorde to the bar. "What's she got out for us to drink today?"

Lorde gestured to the pitcher of pink still left on the counter. "Some girlie drink."

"Some of us like girlie drinks," Liliane said, perching her toned ass on one of the stools. "Fill'er up, bartender."

Lorde wondered if Liliane had been filling up on her way there. He poured her a drink, added ice and prosecco like Morena had instructed him, then found a beer for Richard.

"Cheers," Richard said, raising his glass. "So, how is our girl?"

"Morena?" Lorde frowned. "She's fine."

"Fine?" Richard scoffed. "She lost the man who could arguably be called the love of her life. She's not fine."

"She seemed fine," Lorde retorted, keeping his tone mild. "She was upset when she heard, but she's handling things."

"Of course she's handling things. Hasn't she said anything to you?" Liliane asked, well into her drink.

"I'm not sure what she'd say to me. I'm under the impression that she doesn't know much about how it happened."

Richard waved his unasked questions away. "Emotional, though? Tears? Tantrums?"

Liliane snorted. "From Morena? Please. She's keeping everything inside, just like she always does. I'll talk to her."

"Tia is here," Lorde offered. "I think she came for support."

Richard's shoulders seemed to relax. "Good. That's good. I haven't seen Tia in years," he mused.

"And the last time she didn't seem too inclined to see you, so don't get your knickers in a knot," Liliane said scornfully. "Who else is here?"

"I'm here," said a voice. Lorde turned. The stiffness he'd felt in the kitchen while spying on Jacey in the lobby returned in full force because there was Jacey gliding across the floor with a smile on her face, wearing nothing but one of the inn's thick robes.

"Well, yes you are," Richard boomed as he took a step towards Jacey, gathering her in his arms. Lorde wasn't aware they were such good friends, but maybe Richard was taking advantage of giving an almost naked woman a hug.

She probably wasn't naked. There must be a bathing suit under the robe.

Had to be. Because he was going to explode in his pants if there wasn't.

Liliane stepped up to greet Jacey next and then there she was, right in front of him.

"Hello, Lorde," Jacey said with a hint of a smile.

"Hello, Jacey."

"Is this all the hello I get?"

"What else were you looking for?" he asked with a hint of his own smile, details of their time together coming back to him in very clear images.

"Was I loud enough before?" she asked, biting her lip as she slowly moved up and down along the length of him.

Lorde shook his head. "More."

"That's what I said."

"Then that's what I'll give you." Grasping her waist, he lifted her up so only the tip remained inside her, and then pulled her onto him at the same time he thrust his hips up.

Jacey cried out as his cock slammed against her g-spot.

He lifted her again. "More?" he asked with a raised eyebrow, easily holding her steady even as she squirmed for the feel of his cock again.

"More," she panted. "Please...fuck me like that again."

"If you like."

He held her tight, wouldn't let her move against him. He controlled the thrusts, the depth, and intensity, and Jacey was powerless against his strength.

She gripped his shoulders and pleaded for more, eventually begging for him to make her come. The slow, controlled thrusts were good, hitting every inch of her insides but it wasn't enough. She needed more, friction against her aching clit, desperate for release.

And then he moved his hand between them, his thumb barely grazing her clit, and Jacey screamed. She kept screaming as yet another orgasm raced through her body, and Lorde released her hips and let her hips take what she wanted.

Finally, her body satiated, she slumped against him.

"We're not done yet," he told her, wrapping his arms around her waist.

"Please," Jacey whispered.

"Yes, I heard you begging," Lorde said. In a well-practiced move, he shifted, lifting her from his lap, to turn and lay her on the bed. His cock remained buried inside her. "It'll be over soon."

Jacey groaned as he reared back on muscular arms and began thrusting into her, deep and hard and taking what he wanted from her.

She whimpered as he pulled out, leaving her empty. He pulled her legs up to rest on his shoulders, and driving back in, harder than before.

He thrust in, hard and fast, relentless in his quest keeping his eyes on a point above her head, his shoulder muscles straining. Without a word, without a sound, he fucked her; the only way Jacey could tell he was close to coming was his breath, coming in panting gasps.

And then with a staccato of thrusts, Lorde exploded inside her. His eyes closed, and with a murmur, "Elizabeth," he collapsed on top of her, releasing her legs so they fell on either side of him.

Jacey left him there, his head cradled on her breasts until his breathing slowed and he began to stir.

"That was the best sex in the shortest amount of time I've ever had," she told him quietly.

Lorde raised his head. "Sorry about that," he said, looking anything but.

"I'm not complaining." She laughed. "And because we don't know each other very well, I'm not about to get upset that you said another woman's name when you came. But I think while we wait for round two, you can at least tell me more about her."

"Round two?" Lorde's eyes were wary, from the demand for answers rather the request for more sex.

"You're not getting off that easy."

Lorde chuckled as he rested his head on her breasts again. "You sure did."

Jacey raised an eyebrow, and Lorde chuckled in response, knowing that she was thinking the same thing he was.

"It's good to see you,' he conceded.

"It is," she agreed with a toss of her head, the curls caught up in a clip at the top of her head. "Well, I'm off to the hot tub if anyone cares to join me." With a lingering glance at Lorde, she sashayed to the door.

Lorde heard Richard's sigh.

"I see you're still happily in love with Elizabeth." Lorde turned to Liliane with a question in his eyes. "If you weren't, then you'd be after that girl like a fat kid on a Smartie," she finished with a chortle.

Chapter Fourteen

Gemma

G EMMA'S STOMACH WAS TINGLING with nerves as she made her way down the stairs with Jasper. They'd had a heated discussion about whether to wear a bathing suit; their consensus was to wear one with the possibility of taking it off if that was the norm.

"I'm sorry if this turns into a complete nightmare," she whispered as they reached the lobby.

Jasper squeezed her hand. "We won't let it. Just remember that I love you. And you love me. No falling in love with anyone else."

"We fall in like," Gemma vowed. "Sexual like. That's it."

"Is that even a thing?" Jasper wondered. "Maybe lust?"

"Like doesn't sound as dirty," Gemma whispered as they headed across the gleaming wood plank floor to the bar. The smell of the Christmas tree and the fireplace filled the air with a heady aroma.

"If you're not looking for dirty, I think we're in the wrong place," Jasper whispered back.

"Hello, you two," Morena called from behind the bar. "Headed for the hot tub? Care for a drink to take with you?"

"That would be great," Gemma said too quickly, and Morena smiled knowingly.

"Liquid courage is a lovely thing. I'll fix you another cranberry cosmo. Jasper?"

"Again–great. Thanks."

"Maybe a beer for me," Jasper admitted. "In a really big glass."

"Liliane took out a couple of bottles of wine, so you'll be fine for refills," Morena said, filling their glasses. "You'll like her. And you met Jacey, Dominic, and Tia earlier. They're already soaking in the bubbles."

"Great," Jasper said. Gemma could tell Jasper was nervous by his voice, his posture–ramrod straight–like he expected an attack from behind him. She was tense as well, but at least she had a few days to get used to the idea. She'd thrown it on Jasper only moments ago, and he was doing pretty well for that fact.

"Here you go." Morena pushed the glasses across the counter, only to hold them firm as Gemma reached for it. "I like to remind my guests that they're here to have fun and meet new people, but most of all, relax. No one will judge you for what you might or might not do. The choice is yours. I hope you enjoy yourselves."

"Thank you," Gemma said gratefully. She turned to Jasper, glass in hand. "Let's do this."

"Lead the way."

It was the longest walk of Gemma's life. Not only was the air crisp and cold, but every step felt like there was a weight attached to her foot rather than the cheap flip-flops. Looking around, looking anywhere besides the gazebo straight ahead that housed the hot tub, based on the rising steam and the laughter, Gemma thought that the gardens must be beautiful in the spring. The ground was covered with a thin layer of snow, with the path cleared of any puddles of slush.

"Hey, there!" A glance showed a waving arm from the water. Jacey. And getting closer, Gemma was relieved to see she was wearing a bathing suit.

"Any room for us?" Jasper called in a hearty, booming voice, unlike his usual tone.

"Right beside me," Jacey replied. As they climbed the steps, Gemma noticed how Jacey was smiling at them. She felt her stomach tighten.

You wanted this, she reminded herself. Of course women would want to be with Jasper. What did you expect–that he'd be sitting on the sidelines?

Gemma steeled her back as she slipped off the robe and set it on a nearby chair. Jasper already had a foot in the water but held out his hand to her to help her step in.

"Welcome." The older woman beside Dominic smiled at them as Gemma found a seat beside Tia. "Good idea to bring drinks, but Morena makes sure we have lots of wine. I feel like a third wheel since you all know each other."

"We met when we were checking in," Jasper explained, settling into a spot beside Jacey with a nervous grin pasted on his face.

"We've never been here before," Gemma added, before taking a gulp of her drink.

"And you know what to expect?" Jacey asked carefully, turning to Jasper.

He raised his eyebrows at Gemma. "I do now."

"But not really," Gemma added. "First time for anything like this. Am I allowed to say that?"

"You can say anything you want," Dominic assured her. "Communication is key."

"Then I should say I'm really scared," she admitted, hunching her shoulders. "And completely clueless."

Tia brushed her shoulder against Gemma's. "Don't be scared. No one expects you to do anything you don't want to."

Jasper nodded. "That's what Morena said."

"She is the expert," Liliane said, reaching out of the water for the wine bottle that was just out of reach. Dominic stood to get it for her, and Gemma couldn't help but admire his dripping torso. Stocky but tight, without a hint of a middle-age paunch. She guessed his age to be mid-to-late thirties, at least several years older than her.

Tia was harder to estimate. She was a beautiful woman with catlike brown eyes, and a perfectly shaped reddish-brown bob hanging sleek and straight even with the heat of the water. There were faint lines around her eyes, but her skin was pale and smooth, like she rarely saw the sun without a hat. At least fifty, Gemma decided. And she didn't seem the type to be a swinger.

Not that Gemma had any idea what a swinger looked like, but if she did, it wouldn't be Tia. Tia looked...uptight. Sexy, but severe.

Maybe that was the turn-on. She looked like a headmistress, stalking naughty students with a ruler and a frown.

Gemma turned away, shocked at how the image brought a thrill between her legs.

Liliane looked like a swinger, Gemma decided—laid-back and attractive, with a hand holding her wineglass propped on the edge of the hot tub and the other hidden under the water. From the way Dominic kept shooting glances at her, Gemma wondered if he knew the location of the missing hand.

"So you've never done anything like this before?" Jacey asked again. Gemma shook her head forlornly.

"It's not a bad thing," Dominic hastened to assure her. "Everyone has a first time."

"When was yours?" Jasper asked.

"Yes, what was your first time?" Liliane echoed. "I've never asked."

"Tia has parties," Dominic explained. "And she invited us to one soon after we moved into the neighbourhood. It was...interesting."

Tia raised an elegantly sculpted eyebrow. "That's what you call interesting?"

"It was great." Dominic laughed. "She does the key thing–takes a woman and then picks a man's keys out of a bowl, so it's random."

"Sort of random," Jacey cut in.

"Mostly random," Tia agreed with a sideways glance at Jacey.

"So that first night–?" Dominic spluttered.

"Dominic, really? It was my party. I got who I wanted to."

Gemma gasped with laughter at the expression on Dominic's face. Was this what it was like? They seemed like such good friends. Is that what happened when you had sex with someone?

"I feel like a virgin," Gemma confessed suddenly.

"Touched for the very first time?" Jacey grinned as Gemma recognized the words from the Madonna song. "Oh, thank god. I wasn't sure how old you were."

"I just turned thirty. Jasper is two years older."

"And you've never been with another man? Or a woman?" Tia asked gently, with a glance at Jacey.

"Er...no."

"You're very beautiful, you know." Tia lifted a wet hand to stroke Gemma's cheek. "I love the curls."

"It's...all frizz now." Gemma wished she had thought to pull her hair up like Jacey since the ends of her blonds curls drooped into the water.

Tia smiled, pushing an errant curl behind her ear.

"I think so," Liliane said from the other end of the hot tub. "Might as well."

Gemma felt her eyes grow bigger as she looked from Tia to Liliane, to Jacey who had a smug smile on her face. "Might as well, what?"

"Gemma...would you like to know what it's like to be with a woman?" Tia asked in a gentle voice.

"A woman...you?" Her throat had suddenly closed up so her words were little more than a squeak. "Here?"

"Or in one of the cabins. But I thought here...so you and Jasper could experience it together. It's so warm here in the water." Tia cupped her cheek, drew her forward. "We can start with a kiss. Just a kiss."

And then Tia kissed Gemma, her lips light and soft, wet and warm from the water. So gentle. Gemma opened her lips, felt Tia's tongue slide in, felt the touch echo between her legs like a lightning bolt had struck.

Tia pulled away, leaving Gemma unable to form a coherent thought. "Oh."

"Oh." Tia smiled into her eyes. "What did you think of that?"

"I thought it was nice."

Jacey laughed. "Never tell a man it's nice. Just a bit of advice."

"Not nice. Okay."

"Jasper?" Tia turned to Jasper, who was staring with his mouth hanging open. Gemma recognized the expression from when she had once underdressed in front of him, slowly, with a slow swing of her hips.

She would bet money that under the water, Jasper's cock was hard as a rock.

A frisson of pride began inside of her.

"Is this all right with you?" Tia asked Jasper.

"Uh huh." Jasper's eyes were still wide and staring, and with a laugh, Dominic clapped him on the back.

"First time, bro, first time. There's nothing like it."

"Would you like to take off your bathing suit?" Tia asked. "Liliane, maybe you could help her."

Gentle hands assisted and soon Gemma was divested of her suit, sitting naked and a little uncomfortable in the water. The water was warm and the bubbles hid all of her parts, but what exactly did Tia want her to do?

Tia wanted to kiss her breasts.

Her hand found the warmth between her legs. Gemma instinctively spread her legs, allowing Tia's fingers to press and probe. She rose from her breast, kissing her lips as she explored Gemma's heat.

Gemma gasped against Tia's mouth as her finger slipped inside of her. Softly, slowly, Tia thrust inside, her thumb hard against her nub.

Gemma spread her legs even farther apart.

This weekend was starting to be a really good idea.

Chapter Fifteen

Morena

"ARE YOU WATCHING THIS?"

Morena turned from the window at the sound of Iliya's voice, her face flushing with guilt. She did her best to let her guests do what they wanted to without chaperoning or giving her opinion. She never interfered in their choices, other than to sometimes give couples a nudge at times, always subtly. She never watched, even when something intriguing was going on.

Until now.

"I shouldn't be," Morena confessed, stepping away from the window looking out to the back gardens, giving a perfect view of the hot tub. "I never do."

"You should. Iliya laughed. "This is hot! I've never seen anything like it."

Morena gave Iliya a sideways glance. "I sincerely doubt that."

"Well, maybe...once. But I didn't take part."

"Feel free to join them now."

"No, I think they're doing well enough on their own."

Iliya stepped closer to the window standing to the side so she wouldn't be visible to anyone looking in. Morena reluctantly joined her.

"Look at her face," Iliya marvelled. "I know exactly what Tia is doing to her under the water."

"She's adorable." Morena had been struck by Gemma's freshness when she first met her, worried by Jasper's obliviousness about the inn, but she was happy to see he had figured things out.

Watching your wife get fingered in a hot tub by another woman would do that.

"Looks like the other one's getting in on the action," Iliya said in a hushed voice as Jacey took one of Gemma's nipples in her mouth.

"Jacey doesn't like to wait." The hot tub under the protective gazebo roof was just close enough for her to be able to distinguish faces, but her eyes weren't as good as Iliya's to allow her to see expressions. She could only imagine the look on Gemma's face.

"That's Jacey? And Dominic? I've heard of them." There was no eagerness in Iliya's voice, only a slight resentment. Morena knew her well enough to realize Iliya had a selfish streak that led her to collect as much attention for herself.

Morena suspected Iliya and Jacey would not get along. "Tia is quite fond of them."

Iliya made a soft noise in her throat. "Henry's mentioned them a few times."

"Yes, I believe his parents know Jacey."

"It's so mixed up." Iliya sighed. "Everyone knows everyone else. Almost incestuous."

"Thankfully, it's not," Morena said grimly.

"That's definitely something I've never been into," Iliya agreed. She glanced at Morena briefly, before turning back to the action out the window. "Speaking of connections, how are you doing about William?"

"I should be asking you."

Iliya waved her hand. "It's strange; as soon as Henry and I got together, it was like any pull I had towards William disappeared. I didn't want to contact him. I never thought of him and I never saw him again." Her face fell. "The last time I saw him, I was angry with him. I don't like that. I wish I had time to explain why and what I had been thinking."

"He wouldn't have understood," Morena said in a quiet voice. "No matter what you may have tried to say, he would have gone on believing that you'd be back."

"I always went back to him," Iliya admitted, her hand reaching out to clutch the sheer curtain. "Even with Del, and that was a good marriage. I treated Del horribly."

"I'm sure he's forgiven you."

"I talked to him, the last time Henry and I were in Toronto. He wanted to meet Del–had a total fangirl moment. It was cute."

"Wouldn't Henry have a fanboy moment?"

"It doesn't sound as good. But they're friends now, helping each other with their writing. Very strange. Especially since Kenna can't really look me in the eye."

Morena gave her a sideways glance. "Del's wife? That's too bad."

"I'm glad she's happy with Del, but the lifestyle wasn't for her. Now this one." Iliya leaned closer to the window as Jasper helped Gemma perch on the edge of the hot tub, water streaming from between her naked breasts. "Is that it? No—bathing suit's already gone. That's going to get cold pretty fast."

"I don't think she minds," Morena murmured. "Gorgeous."

"The husband's a looker too. And he's all over the little—Do you see that cock?" Both women focused on the member straining under Jasper's swim trunks. "That boy is going to be popular tonight."

"I think you're a little late," Morena pointed out as Jacey abandoned Gemma for Jasper. "And look, Dominic is getting in on this."

Dominic stood up, his muscular back streaming water and cupped Gemma's cheek. The younger woman looked nervous as Tia moved before her, parting her thighs. "Oh, she's not. Right there? Go, Tia!" Iliya cheered as Tia bent her head between Gemma's legs. "Stop kissing her, Dominic, I want to see her face."

Dominic obeyed, even though there was no way he heard Iliya from inside. He began kissing his way to Gemma's breasts, rosy-tipped with both the cold air and the excitement. Gemma herself closed her eyes, leaning back on her hands as she pulled one of her legs out of the water.

Morena felt a tug between her own legs as they watched them, Tia's head bobbing as she licked and sucked.

Even with the window closed, Morena could tell when Gemma cried out with pleasure, one of her hands resting on Tia's head.

"She's a lucky girl," Iliya said in a hollow voice.

"Yes, she is."

They watched in silence, so focused on the X-rated action outside, neither one of them heard Lorde approach from the other side of the lobby.

"What's that you're looking at?" he asked. Morena leaped back from the window.

CHAPTER SIXTEEN

Lorde

"**H**OLY-WOW.**" LORDE'S EYES WIDENED** as he glanced out the window to see Gemma in the throes in what was apparently a powerful orgasm.

"I bet she's a screamer," Iliya said smugly.

"I don't...need...to know that." Lorde turned away from the sight of Gemma with difficulty. He'd always liked to watch women come, even when he wasn't the one helping with it.

Despite his best intentions, Lorde turned back to the window, well aware of the tightness in his pants. It wasn't right to watch something so intimate, but he couldn't help himself. Especially when Jacey was right there in the hot tub, the water moulding the swimsuit against her full breasts. She straddled one of the guests, kissing him on and on.

Lorde had dreamed about those breasts. But he'd never kissed her. He'd always thought kissing too intimate an action to do with a woman other than Elizabeth.

"Goodness," Morena murmured, her gaze focused on Gemma as Tia lifted her head and kissed her on the mouth.

"I think it's going to be a good weekend," Iliya said, pushing away from the window. "I need to find Henry now."

Morena laughed as Iliya hurried away.

"That doesn't usually happen." Lorde gave the action out the window one last look and reluctantly and turned away. "And so quick. They only just checked in."

"I guess they didn't want to wait. I've noticed things have gotten a bit frisky a few times out there." She smiled at Lorde as the phone rang, hurrying back to the bar to answer it.

Lorde took another peek to see Gemma red-faced and smiling shyly at her audience in the hot tub. It was her first time here, and in another life, Lorde would have been the first in line to make her visit a memorable one. But he had Elizabeth now.

Would Elizabeth ever want to join in?

The thought made him jump like he'd been hit with an electrical current. He turned to find Morena standing there. She'd touched his shoulder, giving him a shock.

"Sorry," Morena said, her hand over the cordless phone. "I have to take this. Could you watch the bar for me?"

"Sure." He shook his head as Morena hurried across the lobby. It was a sign that he shouldn't be thinking of other women. He had Elizabeth–the only woman he'd ever wanted.

The only woman he'd ever loved.

To be truthful, he'd wanted his fair share of women–one who was now currently in the hot tub. Lorde watched Jacey separate from Jasper, with a smile on her face and hair that he could practically feel between his fingers.

Elizabeth. Elizabeth, Elizabeth...

"Do you miss it?" Elizabeth had asked him one night a few weeks ago as they were getting ready for bed. "The other women?"

"How could I miss anything when I have you?" he had replied.

And it was true. Elizabeth was everything Lorde had ever wanted in a woman. There was nothing he couldn't find with her.

But at times, the lure of a new body was tempting. The door to the back garden opened, wrenching him away from his thoughts. "Oh," Gemma said with surprise. "You're not Morena."

"I'm not. Lorde." He moved behind the bar. "Can I get you anything?"

"I came back for more of that cranberry cocktail."

"I've got something you might like better." She was pretty with heavy blond curls, delicate features, and a wide smile. He might have thought the pink cheeks were from the cold run into the inn, had he not seen playtime in the tub. "I see you found your way to the hot tub."

"I..." Lorde tried to hide his smirk as Gemma's eyes widened, so blue and so big, almost like one of Grace's dolls. "Did you see?"

Lorde inclined his head an inch. "Saw what?"

"Oh!" Gemma slapped her hands on her cheeks, and Lorde chuckled. "You did see me...and her. Them. Oh, gosh."

"There's no point being embarrassed. I've seen lots of things going on here."

"Really? Like what?" Gemma said quickly.

"I'm not one to peek and tell."

"Do you kiss and tell?"

"Can't say I'm inclined to do that." He poured her a drink slowly, wanting to keep the conversation going. He had Elizabeth, so there was no possibility with Gemma, but he had to admit she was adorable, and there was nothing wrong with talking to an attractive woman.

"That's what Callie said," Gemma said.

Lorde frowned. "Callie?"

"Callie Champlain. She's a friend of mine. Maybe not a good friend yet, but she's the one who told me about this place, so maybe I should make her a better friend because things are going pretty well so far."

"Callie..." Lorde pictured the voluptuous blonde, recalled sitting beside her at dinner, poised to ask to join her in a cabin.

He'd been *thisclose* with her, and then Elizabeth had been there, and any other woman had been forgotten. "I remember Callie," he admitted. "How is she?"

"She's good. She's part of my book club."

That prompted a laugh. "Can't say I can see Callie in a book club."

"Oh, it's kind of a dirty book club, so she fits right in."

"That she would."

Lorde studied Gemma as he fixed her a drink. The blonde hair was unkempt from the water and Tia.

Tia and Dominic both. And in public. For a first-timer, Gemma was going to fit in very well here.

For a moment Lorde felt a pang of regret that he wouldn't be the one to consummate her first visit. Lead her out to one of the cabins and lay her on the bed, slowly take off her clothes before tying her wrists to the headboard. He liked to do that to the more nervous of the women to take away their control and any doubts they might have.

He had liked to do that. Not now. Now he had Elizabeth, and there would be no tying up nervous women with their big blue eyes staring at him–

"What's in that? Lorde?"

Lorde blinked, realizing Gemma had spoken to him. "Uh, whiskey. Peach schnapps and peach juice with a bit of iced tea. It's sweet."

Like you, he wanted to add.

"I don't usually drink whiskey," Gemma said. "But there's a first time for everything." She stared at the drink, at the tiny umbrella he'd added for her. "I guess there'll be lots of firsts for me this weekend."

"That's what this place is for." Lorde handed her the glass. "Enjoy."

The door swung open and Liliane blew in with a gust of icy air. "Oh ho, I should have known what was keeping you, Gemma. Lorde here keeping you occupied?"

"He's making me a drink. With whiskey." Gemma sipped through the straw, fixing those blue eyes on him.

Lorde felt something stir inside him. "Just a drink."

"Oh, I know. Elizabeth is a lucky woman." Liliane winked. "Would you mind finding me another bottle of wine? We're still going strong out there. Coming, Gemma?"

CHAPTER SEVENTEEN

Gemma

"I CAN'T BELIEVE WE did that!" Gemma giggled for the tenth time since she and Jasper had returned to their room to get ready for dinner.

"I didn't do much of anything," Jasper said. Was that disappointment in his voice? "I mean, Jacey was there and she..." He trailed off with a sheepish grin. "I don't know what I'm supposed to say."

"Dominic said we needed to communicate for this to work," Gemma reminded him as she shrugged off the robe, standing naked in the room. There had seemed little point in putting on a wet bathing suit after Tia had helped her take it off, and the robe was thick and warm and hid everything.

Talking to Lorde while naked underneath had been interesting. He was so good-looking in a hunky, brooding way. So different than Jasper, but Gemma felt her toes begin to curl the more they talked. If Liliane hadn't interrupted them...

"And you want this to work?" Jasper asked. "It seemed like you did, but I want to make sure."

"People saw me," Gemma whispered as she pulled back the quilt.

"Are you planning on going to bed?" Jasper asked.

"I'm trying to warm up."

Jasper nodded. As she watched from beneath the warm quilt, he slipped out of his own robe, peeling off his swimsuit and crawled in after her. Gemma curled up beside him, grateful for his warmth. "And yes, quite a few people did see you. I have to say, Gem, I never would have thought you'd do something like that."

"Are you mad?" She scuttled away from him, gazed at him with horror.

"No! No, of course not. Whatever you want. Whatever you feel comfortable with."

"I didn't know I would have–that they...Tia..." She swallowed. "I don't know how to say it."

"I know what she did." Gemma was relieved to see the smile on Jasper's face. "I was there through the whole thing."

"Yeah."

"It was hot," he confessed in a low voice. "Sexy."

"Yeah?"

Jasper nodded, his hair wet against the pillow. "When you came...I was...with Jacey."

"What did you do to her?" Gemma was more curious about what he had gotten up to under the water than she expected to be. "And what did she do to you? Did you come?"

Jasper shook his head. "I made her come, with my fingers. At least I think I did. She was quiet."

"Unlike me. But you didn't come?" Gemma snaked a hand down Jasper's chest, his taut stomach to find a semi-hard cock. She was surprised at how much she was bothered with Jasper not being satisfied.

"Not in the water," he said awkwardly.

"Probably a good idea. But now..."

"Now we're supposed to be having a shower and getting ready for dinner."

"But there's still time." She pulled away from him, slid farther down under the covers. "It's really warm under here."

"Gemma..."

She grasped his cock, so long and thick. Her husband really did have a magic member. And he knew what to do with it. For the first time, the thought of him being with a woman, him being with Jacey, perhaps, didn't leave her with a tinge of terror.

She felt pride now, at the thought of how he could pleasure a woman. While Gemma was being pleasured by someone else.

"Do you really want me to stop?" Her words were muffled by being under the covers and without waiting for his answer, Gemma took his cock in her mouth.

She heard his answer as if from a distance. "Not really."

Gemma wasn't about to stop, even if Jasper wanted her to. He rarely asked her for a blow job, but she knew he enjoyed them.

And what man would say no to his wife taking him in her mouth?

Gemma used her tongue to explore Jasper while she kept her hand firmly around the base of his cock, sliding it up and down as she licked him like her favourite flavour of ice cream cone.

He tasted clean, albeit smelled a bit like chlorine.

She liked doing this to him, liked it better that he rarely asked. Because it wasn't often, Gemma thought of oral sex as a treat for Jasper. He was always so appreciative.

"Gemma, wait." Cool air bit her back as Jasper yanked the blankets off to the side. She glanced up at him with big eyes, still with his cock in her mouth. "I want to. I saw what Tia did, and I think I should practice."

She pulled her head back, but still kept her grip. "Practice what? Oh!"

Always so appreciative.

Jasper pulled Gemma on top of him so that her hips straddled his shoulders. Without another word of explanation, he pulled her down to him, so that his tongue could explore her secret folds...folds Tia had already explored earlier.

Gemma didn't mind the repeat. "Ohhh," she gasped as Jasper licked the length of her, before probing her with his tongue.

His tongue was almost as talented as his cock. She cried out.

Maybe more so.

She leaned over to take him in her mouth again as his hands gripped her hips.

"I won't take long," he warned, his voice muffled by her thighs.

Neither would she.

Gemma tried to concentrate on his cock–licking and sucking and doing everything she knew Jasper liked, but it was difficult with the sensations he was bringing to her. And every so often, he groaned, the sound sending vibrations through her.

They hadn't done this in a very long time.

They should do it more often.

All too soon, Jasper began thrusting his hips, forcing himself deeper into Gemma's mouth. She continued to keep her rhythm, bobbing as she took him as deep as she could before drawing him out with a lick around the tip and a suck as she took him back in. At the same time, Jasper was devouring her, the talent of his lips and tongue producing cries and moans, choked back by his cock.

Gemma had thought it had been exciting with Tia, but this...It was like she hadn't come in days. Weeks. Sensations roared through her, causing her entire body to clench. She stopped herself from grinding herself on Jasper's open, eager mouth. She wanted more...more of his mouth...that tongue inside her. Flicking against her clit, only stop to suck, sucking so good it was almost painful.

She came quickly, her back rounding as Jasper grasped her hips to keep her down on him, his tongue working to bring her to another climax.

The second one was just as swift, her cries cutting off as Jasper joined her, coming in her mouth with thrusting spurts.

After a moment, she rolled off him. "You really can't do this gracefully," she complained as she awkwardly crawled back under the covers. "I think that was a good practice."

"I agree," Jasper said as he drew her close to him.

"I think this might work out okay." Gemma snuggled closer.

"I agree." He kissed the top of her head.

Chapter Eighteen

Morena

It was a well-dressed and boisterous group who gathered at the dining room table that night. Morena had come late to the pre-dinner cocktail party, but she was proud to find Lorde and Elizabeth reigning over the group, Elizabeth looking beautiful in a flowing black dress, showing a considerable amount of cleavage for her.

Brian stood tall beside her, and Morena caught him glancing at Elizabeth's breasts more than once.

Elizabeth only smiled and shook her hair back, knowing exactly what Brian was doing.

She liked the attention, Morena had realized a few weeks ago. And she was eager to spread her wings. There was no doubt that Elizabeth was madly in love with Michael, but the woman had an itch as well. A need to explore, find herself.

And Lorde did as well. Morena caught sight of him at Jacey's side, the two talking quietly together. The chemistry was obvious between the two of them, but neither Dominic nor Elizabeth seemed to mind.

Dominic had all but glued himself to Gemma's side.

Gemma and Jasper, who had come in late to the party, even after Morena arrived, both flushed and smiling, leaving no doubt in anyone's mind about what they had been up to in their room. She hoped playtime in the hot tub had eradicated any fears in the couple.

They seemed to be enjoying themselves.

"I was beginning to worry that you'd miss the party," a voice in her ear said quietly.

Morena turned to see Coulter beside her.

Jed had taken him back to his house that afternoon, returning just before the party began. Morena had been busy with a kitchen emergency and hadn't had a chance to speak to him. As Coulter smiled down at her with those dimples on full display, she couldn't help but wonder what would happen after dinner.

"It couldn't be helped," she said. "But I'm glad to see it hasn't slowed anything down."

She felt his gaze on her as she surveyed the group and finally turned to face him when it got mildly uncomfortable.

"You're stunning," Coulter said. "And that's not part of a pick-up line. You honestly take my breath away. I don't know how Jed handles it."

"I think he handles it quite well."

"My friend is in love with you. You know that, don't you? Maybe not," he added as her eyes widened. "I haven't seen him this smitten in years."

"Smitten isn't love," Morena corrected.

"Oh, it's love. I'm sure of it."

"How long have you known Jed?" Morena asked him. She glanced around for something to drink–her wait staff should be circulating.

"Let me get you a drink," Coulter offered, taking her arm and leading her to the bar.

"I can–" she began, and stopped as Coulter slipped behind the bar.

"I used to be a bartender," he admitted. "I miss it at times."

"I'm sure the tips were well worth it."

"Definitely." Coulter laughed, the sound lessening the tension in Morena's shoulders. The chaos in the kitchen had caused a stressful few hours. She'd had to deal with spoiled meat; the pork roast Louis had picked up that morning already smelled foul when he had opened the packaging.

Like every other of the misfortunes that had happened in the past few months, Morena suspected Elizabeth's ex-husband was behind it somehow. His cousin owned the butcher Morena used.

For the last time, she vowed.

Luckily, she'd been able to send Eric, one of her new helpers, out to pick up chicken breasts, which Louis had converted into a delicious-smelling chicken marsala.

Morena had been looking forward to the pork roast, though. She was still angry at the spoiled meat.

"What can I get you?" Coulter asked, rubbing his hands together.

"There's another bottle of champagne just waiting to be opened." Morena pointed to the fridge hidden under the counter.

"But before that, would you mind pulling out the bottle of Scotch I hid over there? I could use a mouthful."

This would be for William, Morena decided as she watched Coulter pour her a glass. Without asking, he helped himself to several fingers of the expensive Scotch. "Nice," he said, inhaling his appreciation. "So what are we toasting to?"

Morena had planned on having a private toast to William before dinner, but the problems in the kitchen had prevented it. She had planned to say a few words before dinner since many of the guests had been friends of William's.

She held up her glass. "To old friends."

Coulter clinked her glass with his. "And new ones. I hope we can be friends."

"Why wouldn't we be friends? We have Jed in common."

"We do. But I have the sense you're not warming up to me as quickly as I'd like."

"I just met you!" Morena gave a half-hearted laugh.

"Yes, but you seem to be holding back."

She looked at Coulter, studied his perfect face, how his lips rose in a smile that could literally make her heart stop. He was right. She was holding back. But Morena knew now that it hadn't been because she disliked Coulter–it was the opposite. Knowing what Jed had planned, what he hoped would be happening tonight worried Morena that she might end up liking Coulter *too* much.

Her relationship with Jed was still so new, so fresh, and Morena couldn't bear the thought of something she said or did–or some-one she was with–causing any confusion with their feelings.

But there was no way she could say such a thing to him.

"I'm not holding back," she said softly. "I'm being cautious."

"You're not normally a cautious person, though."

"How on earth would you know that?"

Coulter shrugged. "I used to be a bartender. I can get a good read on people."

"And what do you do now that you aren't a bartender?" Morena skillfully turned to conversation back to Coulter.

"Little bit of this, little bit of that." When Morena continued to gaze at him, waiting for him to continue, he gave another shrug. "I'm between jobs."

"You're a little old for a millennial. Aren't they the ones who don't feel the need to keep a stable job? Although I'm never sure about the ages these days."

"It's not like that." There was a stiffness in his voice that made Morena hold back any further comments.

"What's it like, then?" she asked gently.

"I have a...friend...who likes me to...be available. Whenever she has need of me." Coulter dropped his head as he sipped the Scotch.

"I see."

"Do you?"

"I once found myself in a similar situation." Morena hadn't thought of that part of her past in months, not since Henry had dragged the details out of her when he had written the book. Of living with Simon, an older and extremely wealthy man who had enjoyed having her at his beck and call. He had covered all of her expenses but had offered her no freedom.

Morena had enjoyed the first few months, had suffered through a few more before she had escaped to Montreal.

"Are you happy?" She looked at him searchingly, suddenly feeling her heart open to him. A kindred spirit of some sort.

"I told her I was visiting my parents," Coulter admitted in a low voice.

Morena lifted her glass and clinked it against his again. "Well, then, let's make sure to give you a wonderful weekend, just in case she finds out."

"Will that wonderful weekend include you?"

She sipped her Scotch, gave him a ghost of a smile. "I believe it will."

When they finally took to the table for dinner, Coulter sat at Morena's right, with Jed several seats away. Morena could feel both men's gazes on her as she stood up, wineglass in hand.

"I'd like to say a few words before we partake in yet another delicious feast by my most brilliant Louis." Morena extended her hand towards the chef, who stood at the kitchen door flanked by her help for the evening, Erin and Eric.

"Drink for Louis," Heidi cheered, lifting her glass. The rest of the table followed suit.

"I'm so glad to have such a full table tonight. Some of you are here looking for excitement. " She nodded towards Gemma and Jasper, who smiled with embarrassment. "Some are here because this is like a second home to them."

"That'd be us," Liliane said, hanging her head.

"And some are here because we recently lost a dear friend."

Morena had planned out what to say about William and had scrapped every draft. Instead, she decided to speak from the heart.

"William Burgess was a difficult man to love, but one I was very close to. This was, of course, a long time ago, but William really can be credited with creating the woman I am. At least he'd want to be given the credit for it."

"Yes, he would," Iliya muttered loud enough for Morena to hear.

"I'm not going to stand here and list all of his accomplishments, because it's easy enough to Google that. I'm also not going to try to convince you that he was a saint of a man, because he most definitely was not. More like the devil. But regardless of William's faults, there was something about the man that drew him to us. His spirit or his sense of self—he did throw great parties," she said ruefully. "And that's another reason I'm so glad to see so many of you here. We haven't had a full house in a while. My bank account thanks you, William." Morena lifted her glass. "To finish, I'd like to say how our lives were touched in many ways by William Burgess and he will never be forgotten. To William."

"To William," echoed around her.

"Enjoy your dinner, and play safe," she finished as she sat down, finishing her glass of wine in several mouthfuls.

Coulter held the wine bottle for her as she set down her empty glass. "That was lovely," he complimented as he gave her a healthy pour.

"I hate speaking in public," she admitted under her breath.

"Could have fooled me."

"It stems from being forced to stand up in class every time I answered a question," Morena said, shaking her napkin before setting it on her lap. "Grade five was especially horrible with Mrs.

Ferguson. She'd make you keep standing if you got it wrong. I'm dating myself, aren't I?"

"It's like a mini-history lesson," Coulter teased, with his heart-stopping grin.

"I'll remember that." She laughed.

"So tell me about this William fellow. Notice I used the term "fellow" rather than the more contemporary 'guy'."

"You just keep on with this age thing," Morena marvelled.

"You're the one who makes a big deal about it. I've never been with a woman of your experience and the thought of it turns me on." His eyes twinkled when he smiled. And his dimple was so deep that Morena felt tempted to stick her finger in it.

"Are you telling me I turn you on?" she asked carefully.

"I'd be happy to show you."

Morena turned away from him. "Maybe later."

"Promise?"

"You're relentless."

"You have no idea." Morena laughed as he wiggled his eyebrows. "Seriously, though. Tell me about this William. Jed told me you were close to him."

"I used to be."

"So he must have been a good dude."

"Dude." The word prompted a laugh from Morena. "I don't know anyone who would consider William a dude. No, he was a cruel, manipulative, possessive control freak."

Coulter leaned back. "Wow. Maybe it's a good thing you left that out of your little speech."

"I thought it best."

"So...are you saying you're not into men who are manipulative, cruel freaks?"

Morena sighed into her wineglass. "Not anymore."

"At least that means I've got a chance with you. I'm a *nice* guy." Coulter smiled guilelessly at her.

"You know, I believe you are," she murmured.

CHAPTER NINETEEN

Lorde

LORDE TRIED TO KEEP his attention on Elizabeth during dinner, but they were seated too far apart to talk.

She looked so beautiful in that dress, with the necklace he had given her years ago gleaming against her throat. Lorde remembered the day he had given it to her. The hour. The minute.

It had been the last time he had seen her before he was shipped overseas, where he had spent four years fighting the war in Afghanistan. And back home, Elizabeth had been told that he had been killed by an insurgent's bomb, rather than critically injured. He had lain in a hospital in Germany for months, fighting for his life, only to finally make it back home to find Elizabeth married to Alan and expecting his child.

He had buried his anger under his love for Elizabeth, but at times it flared out. He vowed to keep a tight rein on his emotions tonight, as he watched Brian smother Elizabeth with compliments and flowery words.

Elizabeth didn't need flowery words, but maybe she liked hearing them now and again. She certainly seemed attentive to Brian.

Beside him, Richard had to call his name twice before he was able to pull his attention away from Elizabeth.

"I'm worried about Morena. How has she been since hearing the news?" Richard asked as the salad was set down before him. Unlike Brian across from them, Richard's gaze wasn't fixed on Elizabeth's cleavage.

Lorde shrugged. He disliked gossip and talking about what Morena might be feeling was just as bad. But Richard was one of Morena's oldest friends. "You asked me that earlier. I think she's as well as can be expected."

Richard sniffed. "So she hasn't said anything to you?"

"Not really, no. I asked," he finished defensively.

"I was there, the night he passed away," Richard said under his breath. "I haven't told them yet. Not sure I will. I was in his game room downstairs. He'd gone up with a group to...you know."

"Play?"

"That's what he called it. But he wasn't playing this time. Sometimes he liked to watch." Richard took a long sip from his wine. "He was in his private office watching when he had the heart attack. No one knew. The group finished and came back downstairs. We started wondering where William was."

"And he was..." Lorde may not have liked the man, but he wouldn't wish to die alone on anyone.

"Dead. It sounds like Serena was his latest—she tracked down his housekeeper and got the key to his office. I can't help but think—"

If they had gotten there sooner, would William still be alive?

"Don't," Lorde interrupted. "It's not worth it."

"No." Richard took a deep breath and another sip of wine. "Anyway, that's what happened."

"I don't think either Morena or Iliya need to know the details. Unless they ask. Even so..."

"You're right. Let's do what we can to protect them since god knows William put them through the wringer over the years."

"I thought he was a friend of yours."

"One of my best friends. Doesn't mean I don't think he was a bastard at times. And he didn't always treat women like he should have. Anyway, I didn't mean to get into that with you. There was an envelope with your name on it with his papers."

"You know this because..."

"I'm one of the executors of his estate."

That surprised Lorde. "I didn't know that. You're a lawyer?"

"A very successful one, thanks to William. Which unfortunately is another reason why I didn't open my mouth enough about his treatment of Iliya. Morena too."

"Are you trying to apologize? Because I'm not the one you should be giving that to."

"I know. Anyway, I've got the envelope for you. And a bit of information."

"About?" Lorde had no idea what was in the envelope or how Richard could have any information that would be worth his time.

"A purchase that William made. An insurance company here in Wolfville. Morena asked William to buy it."

"Gibbens Insurance?" Lorde guessed. He shook his head at Morena's deviousness. It was the company Alan worked for. Had most likely been hoping to rise up through the ranks.

"Anyway, William left it to Morena in his will."

Lorde laughed aloud. Morena now owned the company Alan worked for. She'd like that. "What's in the envelope?"

"It's confidential of course, but I can tell you that William had me do a search a few months ago. For a Bram Raspellaire. And an Elena Lorde."

Lorde's throat was dry.

When William had been at the inn a few months ago, he had mentioned to Lorde the possibility of finding Lorde's mother. Lorde had dismissed his claim, knowing William wanted to know everything, to control everything about Morena more than help him find a mother he hadn't seen in years.

Who had abandoned him when he was seventeen, as she ran away with her lover, the man who had been married to Morena.

"I don't want to know," he said firmly.

He hadn't given a thought to the woman who gave birth to him in months. He didn't need her in his life. Morena was more of a mother to him and had been since she'd taken him into her home when Bram and Elena had stolen away in the middle of the night.

The slow revenge she was enacting on Alan only proved Morena's bond with him. Yes, Morena would want Alan to pay for trying to ruin her reputation with the alleged assault, but Lorde knew it was just as much for Elizabeth, and therefore him. Morena protected those who needed it, just like Lorde did.

Across the table, Elizabeth gave a peal of laughter, drawing Lorde and Richard's attention to her.

"You've got a beautiful woman there," Richard said, a forkful of salad poised. "You've made a good life for yourself."

"I have," Lorde agreed. He picked up his glass, gave the ruby liquid a swirl. Once normally only a beer drinker, he'd come to appreciate a nice red wine because of these dinners. Because of Morena. He was the man he was because of her, not the woman who called herself his mother.

He drank deeply from the glass.

"Which is why I need you to burn the envelope," he added. "If what I think is in it, it would only destroy things. *She* would destroy things, just like she did before."

"Unfortunately, I can't do that," Richard said. "I made a promise. But I can keep it safe so that if you ever want it, you need only ask."

"I won't," he said, his voice harsh.

Chapter Twenty

Gemma

"D O YOU KNOW WHO this William was?" Gemma asked Jacey. She was glad Jacey had taken the seat beside her. She would have been happy to have Dominic sit there, but she was nervous about the night to come, and for some reason having Jacey beside her was comforting.

So was the very nice wine she kept drinking.

"I've heard of him, but never met him," Jacey whispered back. "I think we might be the only ones who didn't know him."

"Morena and Tia and Iliya...and Liliane and Heidi...does that mean they *all* knew him. Like...you know, *knew* him, knew him? In the biblical sense?" Gemma tried to keep her jaw from gaping open at the thought but failed miserably.

Jacey's face split into a grin. "I can't believe you used the words 'biblical sense' at this table!"

"You know what I mean."

Jacey raised her glass of wine and glanced down the table at Lorde. Gemma wasn't sure what had happened between the two of them, now or in the past, but from the glances they kept sharing, something must have gone on. "I know exactly what you mean. You get used to you and your friends knowing the same people so...intimately."

"You do this a lot, then."

Jacey leaned forward with another cheeky smile. "As often as I can."

Gemma was amazed at how casual Jacey was about the matter, as well as how proud. Like swapping partners was a normal part of marriage.

But she was right. At this table–this group of swingers–it was.

After she and Jasper had enjoyed each other in their room, they had cuddled, and in the warmth and loving arms of her husband, Gemma had fallen asleep. Jasper woke her up, but it hadn't given her enough time as she would have liked to get ready. After the quickest shower ever, Gemma had gotten dressed in record time.

Being rushed definitely helped with the nerves. Or it might have been the playtime in the hot tub. If she could lose her inhibitions enough to enjoy being...fondled...in public, then swapping partners for a few hours would be easy.

Gemma discreetly adjusted her bra strap. In her rush, she had put on the wrong bra. It made little difference under her purple dress, but she had bought the lacy pink bra and matching underwear, especially for tonight, and it remained upstairs in her suitcase.

At least the panties were still unworn. She'd use them tomorrow night. Because from what she and Jasper had learned that afternoon, they would be doing the whole thing again tomorrow night, but with different partners.

"And your marriage?" Gemma asked cautiously. She had so many questions for Jacey. "How is it? Dominic seems great but doesn't it...wouldn't you...?"

"My marriage is amazing," Jacey told her firmly. "Seriously. No problems with this or this doesn't cause any problems. It's not like we had any major issues before, but starting this, swinging, swapping, sharing, whatever you want to call it, has done wonders for our marriage."

"It doesn't bother you, knowing Dominic...It doesn't bother him?" That was what Gemma was desperate to know. How this worked for a couple like Jacey and Dominic? Young and attractive, in love.

How it might work for her and Jasper.

If they were to pursue it. Pursue the lifestyle, as everyone called it.

Maybe she should just focus on one night at a time.

"You need to be honest and open-minded and shut the door to jealousy or it won't work," Jacey said.

"I have no idea if this is going to work at all. That hot tub might have been a one-time thing."

A handsome, dark-haired man dressed in tight black pants that accentuated all of his assets winked at Gemma as he set a plate before Jacey.

Gemma stared at the plate that he set before her next. Her meal looked restaurant quality–the chicken breasts in some sort of sauce, tiny roasted potatoes and sautéed carrots and Brussels sprouts plated like the top contestant in Master Chef had been working in the kitchen.

"This looks amazing," she said aloud.

"The food is the second-best reason to come here," the man who served Gemma said over his shoulder.

"Look at the ass on him," Jacey murmured, craning to look over her shoulder. "He's new. I'd remember him."

"How many times have you been here?" Gemma asked after taking a quick glance herself.

"Just the once, but we're talking about making it a regular getaway. Not as often as Liliane and Richard, though." Jacey jerked her chin to where the older woman was regaling Jasper with stories. "I think they're pretty close with Morena, though."

"She seems to know almost everyone here but us," Gemma said, sounding a little forlorn.

"She's great and so easy to get to know. It's only your first time and the first night. Plus, she's a little preoccupied with her friend dying."

"The mysterious William. Were they together, do you think?"

"A long time ago. He must have been something if Jed is anything to show for her taste." They both shifted their gaze to Jed, seated beside Iliya. Jed was good-looking in a country-boy type of way, with his easy smile and tanned face, but Gemma was mesmerized by the woman beside him. Iliya was stunning, her model-like face suggesting a few different nationalities in her background, her hair, long and full, with colours ranging from basic blonde to a warm cognac. She looked as exotic as her name. "But what I want to know is, who's Jed's friend?" Jacey murmured.

Gemma hadn't paid much attention to Coulter that evening because he seemed transfixed by Morena beside him, and because he was too pretty for words.

"He's cute," she said in a low voice, hoping the conversations around them would block their discussion.

"Dominic is cute. Coulter is–it's like comparing Tom Cruise and Tom Hanks. Both attractive men, but Tom C. is a little bit more."

Jacey raised her glass and sipped. Gemma couldn't help but stare at her lips, wondering what it might be like to touch them. Jacey had kissed her in the hot tub–at least Gemma thought she did. Things had gotten a little fuzzy when Tia, when her hand…and then her tongue…

It must be the wine giving her those thoughts. But Gemma glanced down the table where Tia was seated on the other side of Iliya.

As if they were aware of her thoughts, both Tia and Iliya turned to smile at her.

Gemma averted her eyes, her cheeks flushing with embarrass-ment. What if they thought she was staring at them? She turned back to Jacey as the woman touched her arm.

Jacey was just as beautiful as the other women at the table, maybe even more so with her caramel-coloured skin and piercing green eyes, not to mention the masses of dark curls now cascading down her back. Jasper had been very complimentary about her.

"Dom and I were talking before dinner. What about giving it a try with us?" Jacey said, sounding so casual, that Gemma took a moment to realize what she was suggesting.

"You? You and...Dominic?" She was so surprised that her voice raised loud enough for Dominic to hear her down the table.

"No?" Jacey asked her own surprise evident in her voice.

"Yes! I mean, sure. I mean, okay...really?"

Jacey shrugged and took another sip of her wine. "As much as I'd like to give Coulter a try, I also like the thought of being your first. First couple, that is. Dominic said as much earlier. Earlier, Jasper seemed like he'd be open–"

"Oh, he's open!" They both glanced down the table at where Jasper was sandwiched between Liliane and Heidi, with another woman leaning over Heidi to touch Jasper's arm. His expression was a combination of excitement and fear.

Gemma thought fear might have been winning.

"I think he'd enjoy that."

Jacey clinked her glass against Gemma's. "I'm sure we all will."

CHAPTER TWENTY-ONE

Morena

MORENA DRANK MORE WINE at dinner than she usually did. Coulter sat beside her, attentive and affectionate, touching her as often as possible. Without talking to Jed, Morena knew Coulter would be joining them that night, and she needed the extra wine to figure out how to deal with it.

The logistics didn't bother her. After dinner, after the others had paired and partnered up and taken themselves to the private little cabins in the woods, she and Jed, along with Coulter, would take themselves to the last cabin on the path, set far into the woods.

Never her room. Morena entertained Jed in her room, and he stayed with her occasionally, but Coulter was a guest, and she never allowed guests in her private space.

It was one thing to share her home with paying guests, but Morena's suite of rooms was her haven, the only place she could escape from being the owner of Mrs. Robinson's B & B. In her rooms, Morena could be Morena, owner of Fallen Gardens, a really big house, and nice gardens.

It wasn't the logistics of the tryst that was disconcerting. She had been with too many men to count. More women than she could remember; threesomes, foursomes, groups...but never had the man she was in love with been willing to share her.

Morena had been part of the swinger community since her early twenties. She'd been married three times, and each time she had made a commitment to a man, she had withdrawn from the lifestyle.

Jed would be the first.

He hadn't told her he loved her, but she thought he might. They'd never said the words to each other, but Morena suspected that was more her fault. She'd never given Jed the opening, changing the subject during the few times Jed had brought up emotions. Feelings. Where the relationship was going.

That had been his latest question to her.

Morena had no idea where the relationship was going after it went to the little cabin in the woods with Coulter. Would it change things?

Jed wanted this. He wanted to share her with someone, a close friend. Jed might be in love with her, and he wanted her to be with someone else.

A first.

During each of Morena's marriages, sharing, swapping, or swinging would not have been an option for her three husbands. As strong and independent as Morena was, her previous relationships had been with men with insecurities, who had taken her love for them and had tried to smother her with it.

Even William hadn't loved her. He might have used the pretty words to manipulate, to make her pretend his feelings were real, but the only person William had truly loved was himself.

Maybe he'd loved Iliya. Maybe a little.

"You look deep in thought." Coulter snagged the bottle of red wine from the middle of the table and refilled the glass Morena hadn't realized she'd drained.

She smiled apologetically. "Maybe a little."

"Can I help?"

Morena bit back her normal response, which would have been that she was fine, that she didn't need help. Coulter was only being kind. Despite how she wanted to keep him at arm's length, the pretty blonde with the dimples was growing on her. "Thank you. Why don't you tell me about yourself to distract me from my deep thoughts?"

"Are you thinking about your friend again?"

"No," Morena said firmly. "I'm really not. So tell me how you met Jed."

"I'd rather talk about you. Jed hasn't told me much." Coulter leaned in close. "He said you were amazing and beautiful and sexy as hell."

"Jed might be prone to exaggerate."

"But he never mentioned the good things, like are your inner thighs sensitive? Or what does it take to make you scream."

Morena took a much-needed sip of wine to moisten her suddenly dry throat. "That's something between Jed and me."

"And me too." He raised his eyebrows. "I hope."

"Is that so?"

Coulter picked up her hand. "He's told you about me?"

"Enough for me to wonder why you're bothering talking to me. You could have anyone at this table."

"I know."

Morena drew back and Coulter smiled. "I'm not that much an ass. I'm new to your group here and I'm single. Plus, I have many interests. And your Lorde over there is off the market, so I'm it for this crowd. But I want you."

"Because of Jed? Because he got me first?" She hadn't meant to sound so blunt.

"You really must think I'm an ass."

"I don't know what to think about you. I know two days ago I didn't know anything about you, and now you tell me you want to sleep with me?"

He leaned in again. "I don't think there'll be much sleep going on. But yes," he said, pulling back and picking up his wine. "You intrigue me, Morena, with your sad eyes and all that gorgeous hair. And I like to be intrigued."

She stared into his eyes. "I'll do my best."

CHAPTER TWENTY-TWO

Lorde

MIDWAY THROUGH DINNER, LORDE left the table to get a few more bottles of wine. The servers were busy in the kitchen and Lorde needed a break from the conversation.

He'd been to many of these dinners and had grown to enjoy them, but down deep, Lorde was a loner and often needed a few minutes on his own to make it through the meal.

He was pulling out the bottles when footsteps sounded behind him. Standing, he saw Jacey walking towards him.

"Can I help you?" From the wide smile on Jacey's face, Lorde thought that might not have been the best question to ask.

"I came to see if there's any of that cosmo left," Jacey said lightly, her gaze studying his face. "The wine is nice, but..." Her smile faltered as she trailed off. "Actually, I saw you leave and decided to follow."

"You followed me?" Lorde set the bottles on the counter, leaned against it. Jacey's hair hung down her back in a wave of curls, her eyes bright and green. She was a beautiful woman, maybe more so than what he remembered.

He remembered what her body looked like after he took off all her clothes. What she sounded like when he touched her, when she came...

"I did. I heard you're not here to play. Just to observe?"

The hint of a smirk on her face made Lorde wonder if she knew of his watching the action in the hot tub earlier. "I'm here for dinner," he said awkwardly. "Just that."

"Too bad." They stared at each other, her thoughts evident on her face. She was thinking of their time together, just as he was.

But he shouldn't be.

"Why's that?" he asked, inwardly groaning as the words popped out of his mouth. Walk away, he ordered. Why are you doing this?

"Why do I think it's a shame that you're not partaking in the availability of the cabins as well as the availability of the guests who would be interested in you?" Lorde nodded. "Because I would have made myself available to you."

Lorde chewed the inside of his cheek. "Is that so?"

"It is. I've thought a lot about you."

Jacey wasn't the first woman to tell him that. Lorde had enough confidence in his prowess to know women enjoying being with him. He always left them satisfied.

But not a lot of them had crawled under his skin like Jacey.

"I think about you when I'm alone." Jacey's voice was low and slightly breathless. "Sometimes at night. Once or twice when I'm with other men. I make myself come by thinking of you."

Suddenly Lorde had difficulty swallowing.

"I came out here to make sure I heard correctly. That you're off the table. That there's no way I'm going to get another chance with you. Because I've got things planned for tonight, but I'd take a pass on them for you."

Her honesty touched him, as well as hardened his cock.

"I–I'm with Elizabeth," he said shortly.

Jacey nodded. "That's too bad. Not for you. I'm happy for you. But I wish..." She smiled at him. "It doesn't matter now what I wish."

"No." He scanned the room, looking anywhere but at Jacey because if he looked at her, he was going to vault across the counter and grab her and pull her back behind the bar with him. His cock was too hard to be comfortable and the only thing that would help was...

"I'll get you a drink," he offered.

"Thank you," she said.

She watched him silently as he made her a drink. His movements were jerky, self-conscious under her scrutiny. Finally, he pushed the glass across the counter, hoping she wouldn't try to touch his hand. Because it was bad enough that she was close enough for him to breathe in the smell of her. A touch might...

"Just so you know," Jacey began as she picked up the glass without any contact. "How good it was between us the last time? Because it was good, you have to admit."

Lorde gave a brief nod.

"If we were to...again...it would have even been better. So much better. And while I am happy you're happy with Elizabeth, I'm not used to getting turned down."

"I'm not turning you down," he protested.

"It certainly feels like you are. But I wanted you to know what you're missing out on." Jacey touched her breast. As Lorde watched, dry-mouthed, she slid her hand into the neckline of her dress.

Her nipples tightened as she fondled herself.

"Maybe you shouldn't..." he stammered.

"Maybe you should do it for me?"

"Lorde?"

Jacey whipped her hand out of her dress as Lorde looked up guiltily to see Erin in the doorway from the dining room, a smirk on her pretty face as her gaze flickered from Lorde to Elizabeth. "Morena was wondering where the wine was."

"I'm bringing it in now." Snatching up the bottles, he tripped over his own feet to get away from Jacey.

"Thanks for the drink," Jacey called after him.

CHAPTER TWENTY-THREE

Gemma

THE KNOT IN GEMMA'S stomach seemed to grow tighter as dinner came to a close. She noticed heads tilted close together as assignations were planned and plotted.

"You okay?" Jacey asked as she noticed Gemma pushing her dessert around her plate.

"A little nervous," Gemma admitted.

Jacey reached for the half-empty bottle in the middle of the table. "Have some more wine. And don't worry, Dom and I will take it easy."

"As opposed to...not easy?"

Jacey leaned closer. "Some like to play a bit. Tying up, a bit of pain. We're not really into that. I mean, I don't mind being spanked now and then, but it's not something I go for."

It was difficult for Gemma to find the words to respond to that. "We're...I don't think...pretty sure we're not into that."

"A straight swap, then." Jacey nodded her head.

"I guess."

Never before had Gemma felt so clearly out of her league.

She caught Jasper's eye at the other end of the table. His eyebrows were raised in an unspoken question. Gemma tilted her head towards Jacey and raised her own brows, showing him four fingers.

Jasper nodded energetically and Gemma smiled.

It was planned. Now all she had to do was go through with it.

"Are you cold?" Dominic asked solicitously as he led the four of them through the woods to the tiny cabin.

"I'm okay," Gemma said through chattering teeth. Didn't anyone wear coats around this place?

"It's right here. We'll get you warmed up," Dominic promised.

There was no leer accompanying his words, nor anything in his voice that suggested anything but concern. That one little sentence managed to unclench the knot gripping Gemma's stomach.

This was going to be all right.

Dominic unlocked the door, and Jacey and Jasper bustled in after them.

"It's sweet," Gemma exclaimed as she caught sight of the tiny room, with the queen-sized bed pushed in the corner and covered with a white comforter. Everything was white except the walls which were painted a grayish-blue, giving the space a sense of peace and tranquillity.

At least the room gave Gemma that sense.

"You're cute," Dominic said, dropping a kiss on the top of her head.

"She really is, isn't she?" Jasper beamed with pride. "And she came up with this idea all by herself."

"You didn't talk about it at all?" Dominic asked.

"No," Gemma confessed. "I didn't even tell him where we were going–that it's a place for swingers."

"That's what I thought when we were checking in," Jacey said.

The four of them stood by the end of the bed, crowding the tiny space. Gemma felt frozen. She had no idea what to do or who to do it to.

After an awkward moment, Dominic took charge. "So, ready to go? No cold feet?"

"My feet are actually really cold," Gemma giggled. Nerves were making her giddy and the last thing she wanted to do was burst out laughing when–

Jacey stepped forward and kissed her.

Tia had kissed her earlier in the hot tub, but Gemma had been shocked into stillness when her lips touched her. This time, when Jacey bent her head, Gemma told herself to relax, to enjoy it.

As her lips moved under Jacey's, Gemma felt her dress being unzipped, slowly being pushed off of her shoulders. She wanted to open her eyes to see who it was undressing her, but she was afraid to find out.

Jasper was close; she could hear the quick intake of breath that meant he was excited. Was Dominic…?

Jacey trailed kisses onto her neck, and Gemma risked taking a peek. Jasper was behind Jacey, possibly undressing her and Dominic...

Dominic's hands were on Gemma's breasts.

She had a fleeting moment of regret that she wasn't wearing her new bra before the bra was unhooked and Dominic helped her take it off.

Then she stood there, with only her panties still on.

That was all she knew until she was on the bed.

A tangle of limbs, hands, mouths. Touching–soft and tentative at first. Deliberate. Could she touch there? Could she look at that? Gemma knew she was stiff and tense because it was painful when Dominic massaged her shoulders when Jacey was kissing her.

"Are you okay?" Jasper whispered. "Is this okay?"

Another man had his hand between her legs, and when she opened her eyes, Gemma saw Jasper's mouth inches above Jacey's breast.

"Yes," she murmured just loud enough for Jasper to hear.

And then it was okay–then it was good, and Gemma's nerves vanished. She was touching *everything,* looking *everywhere,* loving being there with them. Soft murmurs became gasps, breathing became loud in the quiet room, mixed with the sounds of kissing, sounds of wetness. Dominic's fingers inside of her, Jacey taking Jasper's cock deep in her mouth.

It was the best foreplay ever.

And then the frenzy settled and the mood shifted. Jacey lay on the bed between Gemma's legs, kissing her way down her torso. Gemma knew where this was going, knew the fingers were going to be replaced by her mouth, and she sucked in her stomach in anticipation.

In excitement.

She was panting by the time Jacey's mouth found the centre of her heat. Her fingers sunk into Jacey's hair and she tried not to push down. Her mouth–oh, her mouth...and her tongue...

"Oh...yes...yes..."

"Oh, god," Jasper said in a strangled voice. "Look at them."

Gemma arched her back as sensations raced through her at a breakneck pace. She'd always been sensitive, with plenty of erogenous zones for Jasper to play with, but he'd never hit them all like Jacey was doing. Her fingers thrust inside of her while her mouth...oh, her mouth...

"I'm coming," she cried. "I think...I think..."

The wave crashed and crashed again as Jacey continued thrusting and sucking and sending Gemma in a whirlwind over the edge.

Finally, she lifted her head, and Gemma flopped onto the bed like a rag doll. "Your turn," Jacey said to Jasper, beckoning him closer. "I want you in my mouth."

Jacey lay down beside Gemma. "Don't get up," she instructed. "We're not done with you yet."

She rose on her side as Jasper, naked and fully erect, stood beside the bed. Gemma heard the moan of approval in her voice.

"He's got a beautiful cock, doesn't he?" Gemma asked.

"He does." The rest of Jacey's words were muffled as Jacey took him in her mouth, but the sound of her moan came loud and clear, as Dominic knelt between her legs.

"We're not forgetting about you, now," he said, reaching over between Gemma's legs.

Dominic's fingers were slower than Jacey's but more adventurous than Jasper's. Gemma was panting in no time. She wanted...

Moving quickly before she lost her nerve, Gemma leaned over and kissed Jacey's breast, licking the soft skin until she reached the puckered nipple and took it in her mouth.

She'd never touched a woman's breast before, hardly ever seen one, and now she was doing this?

"Fuck me," Jasper muttered.

"Just give...me a minute," Jacey gasped. She pushed Dominic's head deeper between her legs, and he responded by rubbing Gemma's clit.

Gemma glanced up to see Jasper watching her, the heat of lust in his eyes. She smiled and bent to her task.

CHAPTER TWENTY-FOUR

Morena

IT HAD BEEN SEVERAL years since Morena had been with two men, but she remembered very well what to do.

Or what they were going to do to her.

There were hands on her at all times. Lips somewhere on her body. Voices telling her she was beautiful, sexy, hot; that they both wanted her.

Morena tried not to compare them, but it was difficult not to. Jed's touch was more assured, while Coulter's almost tentative at the beginning. His kisses were demanding, though, wanting every bit of her mouth. Firm and wet, tongues exploring, bringing a heat to Morena's core that broke through her inhibitions.

She could have kissed Coulter for hours, lying on the bed, pressed against him.

But it wasn't just her and Coulter in the room. Jed made his presence known, his hands on her body, her breasts, teasing between her legs until she cried out against Coulter's mouth.

As if it was a signal, Coulter leaned away from her, reached for Jed. Morena watched as the men kissed.

Jed's hands tightened on her ass as Coulter deepened the kiss and Morena felt a surge between her legs.

She didn't know if it was arousal or jealousy.

Morena kept watching as they broke apart, watched Jed's eyes as he turned to look at her. She reached for him with hungry eyes, wanting them both for herself. She pulled Jed close, took his thick, jutting cock in her hand.

This was hers. She didn't want to share.

Jed growled as she took him into her mouth, smoothed a hand down her back as she rolled into him. Coulter's lips rained kisses down her neck, his hands gripping Jed's hips to bring him closer. He laid behind her, his own cock hard against her as he covered her hand holding the base of Jed's cock with his own.

And then Coulter's hands were on her body, pulling her leg up so he could reach between her legs, his fingers gentle as they probed the slick heat.

Morena pushed back against him as a wordless plea for more as she took Jed deeper.

And then Coulter was gone, the cool air against her back from where his warm body covered it. Morena still lay on her side, one of her legs propped up–open and inviting. Jed reached over, his fingers searching for her nub.

There was a faint rip of paper and Coulter was back. Holding up her leg, he slid inside her, slowly, carefully like she was a delicate flower he didn't want to damage.

As soon as Morena felt the length of him, she wanted to be damaged.

She wanted to be probed and plundered.

Coulter rocked against her back, thrusting cautiously into her. She moaned with frustration at the pace, the noise muffled by Jed's cock.

"Don't hold back with her," Jed advised, his hands tightening on Morena's shoulders.

"Are you sure?" Coulter kissed Morena's shoulder, bit it gently. She pulled away from Jed. "More," she gasped. "Harder. More."

"I'm going to have to move you." Without another word, Coulter was off the bed, tugging her roughly towards the end, so her legs dangled off the edge. "Tell me if it's too much," he warned, with a gleam in his blue eyes.

"How can it be too much?" Her words were cut off by a gasp as Coulter thrust into her. At that angle, his size filled, stretched, satisfied. He lifted her legs, pressed them against her chest and fucked her.

"It can be a bit much," Jed said as if from far away.

Morena lay back and closed her eyes as the sensations took over her. Coulter was...this was...she felt...

She couldn't think, couldn't form the words. She could only feel.

Jed's mouth was on her breasts, his hand between her legs. For once Morena didn't need the extra stimulation as each thrust from Coulter brought her closer to the edge. She was panting, moaning, crying out without realizing it. With each cry, Coulter seemed to expand, thrust deeper.

She'd never been with a man like Coulter. Morena gripped fistfuls of the blanket as with a scream, Coulter flew her over the edge.

"Oh my god," she said weakly after she'd stopped quivering after Coulter had pulled his magic cock out. Like some kind of drug, Morena already wanted more.

It was as if Coulter could read her thoughts. "Oh, we've got lots more for you."

CHAPTER TWENTY-FIVE

Lorde

L ORDE SAT SILENTLY THROUGH the rest of dinner, refusing to glance at Jacey, even though he was desperate to drink in the sight of her.

Morena was the last to leave the table like she usually was. Lorde wondered if it was because she wanted to make sure things were handled smoothly for those uncertain of the logistics. Erin and Eric had already cleared the table, leaving the kitchen in order before heading out to cabins with Richard and Heidi.

Lorde noticed the new couple, Gemma and Jasper, had gone off with Jacey and Dominic. He looked up to see Jacey give him a coy glance over her shoulder as she left, holding Gemma by the hand.

Elizabeth tugged his hand. "I don't want to go home," she admitted. Her eyes glittered from the wine she'd drunk; no more than usual, but the alcohol seemed to bring out some devil-may-care attitude tonight.

Maybe it had been all the attention she received during dinner.

"Where do you want to go?"

Elizabeth shrugged shyly. "Let's go into the woods. I want to see where everyone goes."

"You've seen the cabins."

"Never when they're in use. Please Michael, just a little walk. It's not like we'd been spying or anything."

He couldn't refuse her and let himself be led out the door towards the garden. From there it was easy to follow the path, the low-lying lights providing enough light for them to see.

"Look at the stars." Elizabeth's head was flung back as she gazed at the dark sky. "I love living here. I can't imagine not being able to see the stars like this."

Lorde glanced down at her and fought the urge to kiss her.

Elizabeth led the way past the hot tub, the water now still and covered. An image of Gemma flashed before his eyes. Lorde hadn't mentioned to Elizabeth what he had witnessed, how he had watched the action.

He'd never done that before. Never known the rush of excitement that drove through him as he'd watched Tia pleasure Gemma. Watched Jacey and Jasper.

He could barely look Gemma in the eye tonight, but he hadn't been able to keep his gaze off Jacey.

The leafless trees closed over them, the branches blocking out the stars. Moonlight streamed through any gap in the trees. The path was still lit by tiny lanterns in the trees, lit earlier by him. He'd checked every cabin for Morena, made sure they were safe and secure for a night of pleasure. It was one of his usual tasks, and he always managed to block all thoughts about what happened in those tiny rooms, never giving a thought.

Until tonight.

Gemma, with her wide eyes and beautiful smile, was even now with Jacey and Dominic. Which one of them would pleasure her first?

What would she sound like? If she had been with Lorde for the first time, he would use the silk scarves to tie her up, and then taken his time learning every inch of her body. He'd discover the sounds she made, and what he needed to do to her to get her to make them. He would–

Lorde shook himself. He was walking hand in hand through the woods with the love of his life, and he was thinking of another woman.

At least he wasn't thinking of Jacey.

If Jacey was with Gemma...Lorde was so deep in thought that he didn't realize Elizabeth had slowed her steps. Stopped between two cabins closest to the path.

"Listen," Elizabeth said in a low voice. "Can you hear?"

"What am I listening to?"

"There. Shush."

Lorde heard a loud cry. A cry of pleasure.

Elizabeth led him off the path, closer to the cabins. The soft crunch of their footsteps on the fallen leaves blocked all sounds. But when they stopped, closer to the first cabin, he heard the cry again. Louder.

Elizabeth reached on her tiptoes, to whisper in his ear. "What do you think they're doing?"

The warmth of her breath against his neck made his cock stiffen. Or maybe it was the low growl from the cabin.

He didn't recognize the voice. Didn't want to. He preferred not to have a face to go with what he was imagining happening in there.

He pictured a woman on the bed, a man above her, driving into her. Her legs wrapped around his waist, her wrists pinned to the by strong hands.

Lorde realized Elizabeth was watching him. Could she tell what he'd been thinking? The slow smile she gave him suggested she did.

So did the hand reaching for his belt buckle.

"What are you doing?" he hissed as with a quick move, she had his belt undone in record time.

"What do you think I'm doing?"

"But...here?" Her hand was down his pants, the thin fabric of his dress pants doing nothing to keep out the chill from the air. If Elizabeth's hand was anything to show for it, she should be freezing in her dress, the breeze whipping the skirt around her legs.

Legs wrapped around his waist...

"Why not here?" She gripped his cock with a cold, but firm hand.

"But–"

"Do you want me to stop?"

Lorde could only shake his head, which prompted a satisfied smile from Elizabeth. Still with her hand wrapped around his cock, she tugged him farther into the woods and positioned him with his back against a tree, hidden from view of the path, but still within hearing distance of the cabin.

Where things seemed to be heating up.

The cries rang through the trees at regular intervals. Lorde leaned against the tree, the bark rough through his shirt, as Elizabeth stroked him.

What was she doing? Did she bring him out to the woods with this plan or did hearing others' lovemaking turn her on as much as it did him?

He had no idea it would have excited him this much.

In the cold, darkness, her hand warmed as it slid up and down his cock. Did she think–What was she thinking?

Without a word of warning, Elizabeth unzipped him fully and bent her head, taking his cock into her mouth.

Lorde drew in his breath with a hiss.

Warm and wet; she kept her hand on the base of his cock as she licked and sucked, bobbing her head slightly. Lorde breathed deeply as the feel of Elizabeth's mouth blocked out the cold and dark. Blocked out everything.

Except for the cries from the cabin.

There were more than two voices. Lorde couldn't help but picture Gemma and Jacey. Both of them together...watching Jacey pleasure Gemma as Lorde drove into her, gripping her hips tightly.

Whoever it was, they were vocal. And demanding.

"More. Please...more."

He touched Elizabeth's head, her blond hair falling in sheets over her face. With a sweep of her arm, she pushed her hair back, gripped his cock a little tighter.

Lorde pictured thrusting into Gemma, her tightness gripping him as strongly as Elizabeth. A cry rang through the night and another.

It was as if Elizabeth was being urged on by the unseen cries. She took him deeper, her tongue circling his tip, and Lorde stifled his own groan. He arched into her, fought the urge to push her head, for her to take him even deeper.

She moaned, and Lorde's eyes rolled back into his head.

Thoughts of Gemma and Jacey and any other woman faded as he gazed down at Elizabeth, thought of how lucky he was.

Lorde could hear his own breathing as Elizabeth brought him closer. So close...so good. With a deep groan, he came into her mouth, without hearing the last harsh cry of pleasure from the cabin.

Chapter Twenty-Six

Gemma

GEMMA LAY CURLED ON her side and watched Jasper as he slept.

His lashes were long enough to brush his cheeks, the envy of all women who knew him.

Now, another woman knew him.

She closed her eyes as the image of Jacey and Jasper invaded her thoughts. Gemma had looked over only once as Dominic made love to her–twice. Jacey had been astride Jasper, riding him like a racehorse. Jasper had been staring up at her with lust in his eyes and his hands full of her breasts, so much bigger than Gemma's.

Lust, not love, Gemma reminded herself. Just because he made love to someone didn't mean he loved her.

Could it be called making love? Maybe calling it sex was easier. They slept together, even though Gemma had been the only one to fall asleep.

They had *fucked*.

Gemma inwardly cringed. She hated the word but had to admit, it was a good fit. Dominic had fucked her; Jasper had fucked Jacey; Jacey had fucked Gemma while the boys had watched.

There had been a lot of fucking going on last night. Maybe she should get used to the word.

What would happen that night? Would they go with Dominic and Jacey again? Would it be someone else?

Jasper shifted in his sleep. Gemma leaned closer. She had been waiting hours for him to wake up, so she could talk out the thoughts whirling in her head.

They had *fucked* other people.

"Wake up," she whispered. Obediently, Jasper's eyes fluttered, blinked open, closed again. He reached out with a long arm to pull her close.

Then stopped, his hand resting on her hip. His eyes flickered open.

"Are we okay?" The urgency was evident in her hushed voice.

Jasper closed his eyes, and with a smile, pulled her close. "I think we're fine."

"Did you have fun?"

His eyes opened fully. "That's almost as silly as me asking you if you had fun."

"I guess so." Gemma rested her head on his chest, feeling his heartbeat as she stared across the room. Morning sun eased through the curtains, falling to the floor in ribbons. Slowly, Jasper's breathing deepened.

"You can't go back to sleep," Gemma said, giving him a poke.

"Why not?" he muttered.

"Shouldn't we talk about this? Compare notes. Find out how we're feeling?"

"I'd like to go back to sleep."

Gemma reared back with exasperation. "Jasper!"

Jasper shifted and with a yawn, blinked his eyes open. "Gem, we can talk if you need to, but I'm fine with this. It was something you wanted to try."

"We," Gemma corrected sharply. "Don't say it was just me."

"I'm trying to give you credit. It was your idea, and it was fun. A lot of fun. More fun than I could have ever imagined, and that's because you were brave enough to book this place. And I'm fine with it all. If you have a problem–"

"I don't. I have to make sure you don't."

"Well, I don't. Except I'm really tired, and I'd like to get more sleep before we get up and do the whole thing again."

"You really want to do it again tonight?"

Jasper smiled at the eagerness in her voice. "As long as you're fine with it. Of course, if you'd like we could stay holed up in our room all night."

"No," she said quickly, too quickly. Jasper chuckled.

"That's what I thought. But maybe we could take a break from the hot tub? I'm never going to be able to be in one without thinking of you..."

Gemma smiled and cuddled closer. Neither was she.

CHAPTER TWENTY-SEVEN

Morena

MORENA WATCHED JED SLEEP, his lashes so long and fair that they grazed his cheeks. He lay on his stomach, his face turned towards her, the covers having slipped down to leave his muscular back bare. Morena was tempted to pull them back up to stave off the cool morning air but didn't want to wake him. He would have to be up and back to his farm for early morning chores soon enough, but she wanted to let him sleep just a little bit longer.

They had come back to her room last night, leaving Coulter at his door on the second floor. Morena was glad to have some distance between them.

The cabin had been good. There had been no doubt about that. Coulter was...talented in many, many ways. Morena awoke sated and with a smile on her face.

But now watching Jed beside her, so warm and content with him in her bed, Morena had a different sort of smile on her face.

As if he knew her thoughts, Jed's eyes fluttered open. A sleepy smile crossed his face, and he reached out an arm for her as he rolled onto his back. In one easy move, he had her tucked into his side.

"I love you," he said in a sleep-clogged voice.

"I love you too." There was no reaction to her words for a moment, and then Jed's eyes popped, fully awake. "I love you," Morena repeated in a whisper.

It was the first time she had said the words.

Jed closed his eyes and snuggled her closer. "I'm glad."

"That's almost as bad as thank you."

Jed chuckled. "Which is how you responded the first time I said it."

"I was hoping you'd forget."

"Never."

The whirr of the ceiling fan was the only sound in the room. "I have to ask," Jed began. "Why say it now, after a night spent with my best friend?"

Morena bit back her giggle. "Seems inappropriate," she admitted. "But it was time. Last night just showed me that."

"How was it for you?" Jed asked hesitantly.

"Do you really have to ask?"

"I mean...you didn't...You seemed unsure when I first mentioned it."

Morena considered her words. "I don't want to share you."

Jed craned his neck to look at her. "What exactly does that mean?"

"It means I don't want to share you with anyone. In the past, and you know my past, I've never been in a relationship with a man I truly cared about, and I think it's because I don't want to share. If you want to do this, that's fine, but not with me in the room."

Jed frowned. "I still don't understand."

She smiled, shifted so she could look at him. "I wouldn't be able to handle you with another woman. Watching it. Last night when Coulter kissed you, I couldn't even enjoy how sexy it was because all I could think was that *I* should be the one kissing you. So if it happens, fine. We can try that. But not together. You with someone, and me with someone. Separately."

"Okay, okay. I get that. But is this what you want?"

She sighed. "I may love you, but I don't know if that means I'm ready for a monogamous lifestyle. I tried that with all three of my husbands and it never worked out. I thought that when you love someone, you should forsake all others. Maybe with you, maybe I shouldn't. Maybe it would make this last."

"I'd like this to last."

"I would too."

Jed rolled on top of her, his hand pulling up the bottom of her nightgown. "I'd like this to last too, but I don't really have time. Plus, I can't stop thinking how sexy you were last night.

She smiled and spread her legs as she felt his hard cock against her thigh. "We have lots of time for that."

Morena was tired as she took her usual spot in the kitchen to help Louis serve breakfast. Not everyone showed up; the fact that Fallen

Gardens was called a bed and breakfast was an anomaly. Dinner was the most important meal at the inn, as that was where the action happened.

The action happened in the cabins in the woods, but dinner was where it usually started. People grew comfortable with one another, made their choices.

Would Morena have chosen Coulter last night if she had had a choice? Because the option had been taken out of her hands when Jed had expressed a desire to join in the festivities. That had been one thing, but when he said he had a friend...

Morena arranged the warm muffins in a basket, set it on the counter. She was acting like she didn't have a good time last night. Coulter had been...

She closed her eyes and turned away from Louis. There was no way he could tell her thoughts, but if he could...

For the first time, Morena wondered what Louis thought about all of this. That he worked at an inn where sex was a free-for-all. Louis was happily married. If not, Morena wondered if he would be interested in joining in, like the girls did. And Eric, her latest find.

Morena glanced up as Coulter walked into the kitchen, looking as fresh and rested as if he got a full eight hours of sleep last night.

He didn't. Not even close.

Coulter slid onto a stool at the counter and smiled at Morena. Something melted inside Morena at the sight of his dimples. "Morning."

"Good morning, Coulter," she replied primly.

"Good morning," he echoed, his smile widening. "And how did you sleep last night?"

"Just fine, thank you." He smirked. "And you?"

"Like a baby."

Maybe it was his age. Morena could remember nights in her twenties and thirties when she had fallen asleep just before dawn was breaking, only to wake up hours later, raring to go.

Oh, to be young again.

As Louis made pancakes for Coulter, other guests began to slowly drift in. Most settled in the dining room and Morena spent most of her time running between the two rooms, ferrying plates and coffee refills. She felt Coulter's eyes on her every time she returned to the kitchen, tightening the anxious knot inside her.

Why was she reacting like this? She'd been with men as good at pleasuring her as Coulter had been—some even better. Why was Coulter getting under her skin, like a rash she itched to scratch?

She'd never shared someone she was in love with.

The realization came about halfway through the breakfast rush and literally made Morena come to a full stop in the kitchen.

"Are you okay?" Coulter had been watching her again, noticed the expression on her face.

"Fine," she said shortly. Why hadn't she thought of that earlier? In all of her three marriages, Morena had never once been involved in a swap with her husband. And serious relationships had been few and far between in recent years, as Morena preferred to keep things simple by joining in with established couples.

Would this work with Jed?

She'd find out after tonight.

CHAPTER TWENTY-EIGHT

Lorde

LORDE AND ELIZABETH SPENT most of the day at home. It was quiet with the girls being at Alan's, and Lorde missed hearing their voices.

"What do you think they're doing?" he asked for the fourth time as they were dressing to go back to the inn.

"They're having a great time," Elizabeth assured him. "As much of an ass Alan was to me, he was a good father to the girls."

"I know."

"Did you ask Morena about Beth?" Elizabeth asked as she fit a dangling earring in. She wore a short, fitted velvet dress that left her shoulders bare.

Lorde's breath had stopped when he had first seen her.

"She won't admit to anything," Lorde said. "She pretended to be surprised when I told her we'd seen them together, but not upset about it. Which tells me she knew about it."

"But...why? Do you think she somehow set them up? And why? She knows what he did to me, doesn't she?"

"That's the whole idea," Lorde exclaimed. "I can only think Morena is trying to set up Alan, and using Beth to help her. It makes sense. Beth looks a lot like you and even has the same name. If Alan has a type, it would be her." He pulled his shirt from the hanger and put it on.

Elizabeth stilled as she fumbled with the clasp on her necklace. "For me?" Elizabeth whispered.

"Of course for you. But for her too. She's still mad about that mess with being dragged into the police station." Leaving his shirt unbuttoned, Lorde moved behind Elizabeth and fastened the necklace.

He took a moment to breathe in her scent, floral with a hint of citrus.

"Which Alan was responsible for," Elizabeth continued, smiling her thanks.

"We don't know that."

"Oh, yes we do," Elizabeth said grimly.

"Okay, we do. Morena doesn't take things like that lying down."

"I never knew she was so vindictive." Elizabeth shivered with delight.

"I don't know if I'd use that word. She likes to take care of her own."

"She's like a mother to you."

Lorde turned away. "More than my own was."

Elizabeth moved into the ensuite washroom, once so bare and stark, but now filled with creams and lotions, most of which Lorde had no idea what they were for. It even smelled like Elizabeth.

"You looked like you were having an intense conversation with Richard at dinner last night," she called to him, rummaging through a drawer.

"Mm-hmm." Lorde fingers fumbled with the buttons. He had hoped Elizabeth wouldn't ask, hadn't noticed, but he should have known better. Elizabeth didn't miss much at Morena's dinners.

Elizabeth stood at the door to the bathroom with a mascara wand in her hand. "Is that all you're going to say about it?"

"Nosy, aren't you?"

"You have no idea."

"It was about William," Lorde admitted with a sigh. "I had no idea he was William's lawyer." He paused, uncertain about how much he could tell her. It was Morena's business, and as much as he loved Elizabeth, he did have loyalty toward the older woman.

"I don't have to know if it's about Morena," Elizabeth said quickly as if she sensed his indecision.

"It is, but...there's stuff about Alan too."

"Alan?"

"William was very...protective towards Morena. After that mess with Todd Thompson and Alan's connection, it seems like William was looking for a little revenge."

Elizabeth's eyes were wide. "What did he do?"

Lorde searched her for anger, for indignation, but found amused satisfaction. "Apparently he bought Gibbens' Insurance."

"Really. He bought the company Alan works for. That seems a bit suspicious."

"And left it to Morena. So now she owns the company."

"That Alan works for," Elizabeth finished gleefully. "That's priceless. She can have him fired in a minute."

"Sure, but what's that going to do to you? We worked hard to get the separation agreement signed."

"That's true." She heaved a disappointed sigh. "What's Morena going to do?"

"I don't even know if she's heard. She told me the reading of the will wasn't until next week. I think she and Iliya are going back to Toronto for it."

"It might be fun for her to hold something over Alan's head."

"Fun for you, you mean."

Elizabeth grinned at ducked back into the bathroom, standing before the mirror to touch the mascara wand to her fair eyelashes. Lorde followed her in, watched intently as she finished with her eyes, choosing a lipstick from the selection cluttering the drawer.

Why did she have so much makeup? She was beautiful enough without it.

"William knew something about my mother," Lorde blurted out.

Elizabeth's gaze met his in the mirror. "Your mother? How?"

"Because of Morena. I'm sure he tracked Bram down, probably without her knowing."

"If Morena knew where your mother was, she would have told you. She wouldn't keep that from you," Elizabeth was quick to assure him.

"It wouldn't have made any difference. My mother wanted nothing to do with me. That was clear when she left without a word." The bitterness was still there. Muted, and distant, but still there.

"Michael, have you ever wondered if maybe she couldn't have come home?" Elizabeth asked in a quiet voice. "To leave without a word–to never come home? Maybe…maybe she couldn't. Maybe something happened to them."

Lorde stared at her reflection, mulling over Elizabeth's words. It had been something that had crossed his mind once or twice, pushed away by his anger, by his need to blame his mother. He needed to hold her responsible for abandoning him.

"It doesn't matter," he said finally. "She's dead to me."

She turned, touched his shoulder. "You can't say that."

"I can because it's true. I don't want to talk about it." Gripping his emotions with an iron fist, he turned back to the bedroom. "Talk about something else."

Elizabeth gives a strangled laugh. "The only thing I want to talk about is something you won't want to, so we might as well finish this."

Lorde shook his head. "There's no point. Really–I'm fine. I've lived with the fact that my mother left me for over half of my life and there's no sense wondering about it now, especially when things are going so well with us. I don't need her, not that I ever did."

"I don't believe you, but okay."

He tucked in his shirt, standing so he could watch her apply lipstick, a creamy rose colour that made her lips seem fuller. "What's this that you want to talk about that I don't. How do you know what I don't want to talk about?"

A quick change of topic was best. Distract Elizabeth so she wouldn't start to press, to probe.

"How many women have you been with?"

Lorde blinked with shock. That was the last question he'd expected.

"A lot, right?" Elizabeth continued as she stepped back into the bedroom. "I can only guess. I've only been with two men in my life. Do you think that's fair?"

"I'm not sure if fair is the right word. I've never been with any men, if you want to look at it that way."

Elizabeth frowned. "Don't joke about it."

"It's not a competition." Lorde paused to rethink his words. "Do you want another lover?"

"No, of course not."

"Then what?"

"I don't want a lover, like an all-the-time, lover. I only want to be with you. But at Morena's, what everyone does over there—"

Lorde's heart stopped.

"I'm curious."

He turned so she couldn't see his expression. How could something make him so fearful and yet fill him with excitement and longing? "Is that the same fear of missing out on things that people have about Facebook?"he asked, trying for casual.

"No. Maybe." She paused long enough for him to turn back to her. "Am I missing out?" she whispered.

"I can't answer that."

"I want to know. I think I might be."

Lorde sat down on the bed, shoulder slumping. Why did he feel this was the beginning of the end? Elizabeth had always been curious, but this seemed more, and he loved her to much to stop her. "I don't think I could handle knowing you were with another man," he said honestly. "I know it's selfish and sexist and a bunch of other things, but Elizabeth...knowing you were with Alan all those years...it nearly did me in. If you were in a cabin and I was right across the path–"

Elizabeth jumped at his words. "What if you were in the cabin with me?"

"I think that'd be worse."

She was silent as she ducked into the walk-in closet that he had cleaned out for her when she moved him, getting rid of years of clothes and shoeboxes to make room for Elizabeth's things. Lorde wanted to heave a sigh of relief. Elizabeth wasn't going to push it, wasn't going to make him make a decision that night, not when Jacey and Gemma would be at the table, both tempting him in their own ways.

"What if it wasn't a man with me? What if it was a woman?" Elizabeth's voice drifted out from between the clothes.

"What do you mean?"

"I'm curious about that too."

His throat dried out as he pictured the scene. "You want to be with a woman?"

She poked her head out of the closet. "Maybe. I don't know. I know I want...I don't know what I want."

Lorde couldn't answer and with a rueful sigh, Elizabeth returned searching in the closet.

Another woman. Lorde had been with two women more time than he could count. Seeing Elizabeth with a woman would be...

"Maybe that would work."

Silence greeted his words. Slowly, Elizabeth backed out the closet, shoes dangling from her hand. "Really?"

CHAPTER TWENTY-NINE

Gemma

"I love Christmas!" Gemma exclaimed. "I can't believe we get to decorate this gorgeous tree."

"I can't believe there aren't more people down here." Dominic handed her a glittery ball.

"More decorations for us," Coulter said.

Jasper was still in their room, but Gemma was too excited to wait. Last night–yesterday–had been more than she could have ever imagined, and she couldn't wait to see what the night held. She had dressed quickly but with care, her choice being a dark red fitted dress that swirled around her knees.

She felt pretty and desirable as she went down the stairs, even as her stomach clenched when she saw Dominic with Coulter in the lobby next to the huge Christmas tree.

Gemma had had her share of big Christmas trees, all found and cut by her father, but none had reached the twelve-foot height of Morena's tree.

"How are we supposed to reach the top?" Gemma wondered as she reached the bottom of the stairs.

"I'm going to put you on my shoulders," Coulter said with a grin. Gemma's stomach unclenched and proceeded to flip over.

Coulter was the best-looking man she'd ever seen, a mixture of Chris Helmsword, Chris Evans and Chris Pratt—all of her favourite superheroes. His blue eyes sparkled like the lights on the tree.

"I don't think I'm dressed for that," she said in a shaky voice.

"Oh, I think you're dressed perfectly." Coulter laughed.

"Even better for climbing a ladder," Dominic pulled out the step ladder hidden beside the tree. "We can look at those sexy legs up there."

"Why do I have to be the one to climb the ladder?"

Coulter and Dominic shared a glance. "So we can watch you," Dominic said with a wink.

She relaxed at the wink. Gemma hadn't seen Dominic since they had walked back to the room. It was strange to talk and laugh with a man who had seen her naked—more than seen her naked. Who had touched her, and watched her with his wife, and knew what she felt like.

His cock had been inside of her last night, and this was the first time she had seen him today. Would it be easier if she didn't see him?

Had Dominic liked having sex with her?

"But first, a drink." Coulter headed to the bar and Dominic smiled at Gemma.

"How are you today?"

"I'm good, thanks. And you?"

"Everything okay after last night?" he probed.

"Oh, that. Sure, everything's fine. I'm sure it's no big deal for you; you and Jacey do that all the time."

Dominic frowned. "Of course it was a big deal for me, especially when it was your first time. I wanted to make sure –"

"Did you like it?" she blurted out. Did she really say that out loud?"Did you like having sex with me?"

That made it even worse.

But Dominic didn't laugh, didn't look offended. He stepped closer and cupped her cheek in his warm hand. "It was amazing," he said in a low voice, staring into her eyes. "One of the most enjoyable nights of my life."

"Are you just saying that?" She held her breath. Take a compliment for once, Gemma, she begged herself.

"Of course not." Dominic leaned closer. "*You* were amazing."

"I was? So were you," she hastened to add.

His hand slid to her waist and he pulled her closer. For a giddy moment, Gemma let herself believe she could feel his hardness against her thigh. "Do you know what, Gemma?"

"What?" she whispered.

He glanced up. "There's mistletoe up there." And then he kissed her, not a chaste, friendly kiss but one with heat and passion. One with open mouth, with tongue and which made Gemma's toes curl inside her pointy-toed shoe.

"What's going on over here? I was just gone for a minute and you move in on my girl?" Coulter's voice broke them apart, sending Gemma staggering backwards at the surprise of the interruption. Dominic reached out to steady her.

"Just taking advantage of the seasonal perks," Dominic said easily, giving her a wink as he took a glass of champagne from Coulter's hand.

"Ah, mistletoe. Don't mind if I do." Coulter set down the glasses and swept her into his arms.

Gemma caught her breath at the swiftness, at the intensity in Coulter's gaze. But when he lowered his lips to hers, it was to press gently against her mouth, and then he pulled away.

"I forgot to ask if I can kiss you," Coulter whispered.

"You don't have to ask," Gemma said in a shaky voice.

"I do. So–yes?"

"Yes...please."

And for the second time in as many minutes, Gemma was thoroughly kissed.

Kissing Coulter was a revelation. His mouth moulded to hers and took control. Her lips parted, his tongue plundered. He dominated her.

Coulter kissed her on and on, and Gemma forgot about Dominic until he cleared his throat.

"Okay, we've got a tree to decorate. More kissing later," Dominic said with a slight edge to his voice.

Coulter kissed her one last time, softly, sweetly and pulled away with a smile on his perfect face. "Promise?"

Gemma's whole body was tingling as she helped Coulter and Dominic begin to place the ornaments on the great tree. Dominic did make her climb the ladder to place baubles on the upper branches, both him and Coulter taking the opportunity to slide playful hands under her skirt.

Coulter kept refilling their champagne glasses, so by the time other guests came down to help, she was buzzed with a smile that wouldn't go away.

"Having fun?" Jasper asked with a grin.

She hadn't seen him come down the stairs. "I am. I–" She didn't know how to express how she was feeling to her husband, didn't know if she should.

Jasper leaned forward to kiss her. "Coming here was a good idea, wasn't it?"

"It was," she agreed with a wide smile.

CHAPTER THIRTY

Morena

M ORENA DRESSED WITH CARE that night.

Not that she didn't every night, but that night she wanted to make an impression. So the little black dress came out of the closet, the one with the diamante strap that slashed over one shoulder and left the other bare, the one with the ruching that both clung to her curves, yet hid everything that needed to hide. Her *I feel sexy* dress.

She did feel sexy. She'd had fun last night and was looking to do so tonight. Only it wouldn't be with Jed and Coulter again.

No, tonight Morena was picking a man for herself.

Jed would be paired off with someone as well. Morena knew there was no denying that the females in attendance at tonight's dinner would be lining up for him, salivating at the thought. This would be his first cabin visit without her.

Morena pushed any envious thoughts out of her head and focused on how a little excitement with others would no doubt help their relationship.

Not that their relationship needed help. She'd made sure of that this morning.

Morena fastened her dangling ruby earrings when the knock came at her door. She was almost ready to join the tree decorating party in the lobby, on time for once.

She opened the door to find Richard, impeccably dressed in slim-cut black pants and a dark grey shirt at her door. "Richard! And Iliya." Iliya stepped from behind Richard, dressed like Morena, in black.

On Iliya, with her hair and lovely figure, it looked far sexier than Morena's reflection in the mirror.

"You look lovely as always," Richard said smoothly. "Can we have a moment before you go down?"

Morena frowned, matching the expression on Iliya's face. "What's going on?"

Richard sighed as he glanced from Morena to Iliya, pushing his way into the room. "It's nothing bad, but I'd rather not have this discussion in the hallway."

"Sounds serious." Morena closed the door behind them, noticing as they glanced around her suite of rooms with wonder. One of the first things Morena did when she set up the property as a bed and breakfast was to make a space for herself, for privacy and somewhere to escape from the guests in her home. Other than the weekends booked for the crowd, most of her business came from tourists eager to explore the Maritime provinces. For those guests, she provided a bed and a full breakfast, but other than that, her time was her own for the rest of the time they stayed at the inn. Rather than be underfoot for those touring the gardens, reading in the library nook in the lobby or strolling through the woods, she escaped to her rooms.

A small living area with a television and office space, with shelves and shelves of books; a small kitchen area for when she couldn't be bothered to head down to the kitchen and finally a huge bedroom, with floor-to-ceiling glass, giving her third-floor room a perfect view of the Bay of Fundy. A sliding room led to a terrace as large as her sitting room.

"This is incredible," Richard marvelled with his gaze fixed on the view. "I've never been up here."

"No, I like to keep this private," Morena said pointedly, moving forward to sweep her rejected jewelry back into the velvet-lined boxes that held it, and then back into the safe in her closet.

One couldn't be too careful when one had people wandering through one's home. Morena kept the door locked, but after one curious guest showed up in her room one afternoon with the pretense that they were exploring, Morena had kept anything special to her locked up.

"I can see why." Iliya's attention was on the bed; the wide, vast expanse of white looked like an island against the never-ending blue of the room. Pillows were stacked against the white satin headboard. "It's beautiful."

"Thank you. Why are you here, Richard? I need to be downstairs to see to the party. After missing most of it yesterday with the kitchen escapades..."

"Of course." Richard turned from the window with apparent reluctance. "It's about William."

Morena stared at him, wondering what could be so important for Richard to come here, to invade her rooms. Couldn't they have this conversation downstairs, in a quiet corner of the lobby, with a drink in hand? In the back of her mind, she was cringing at the thought of William still attempting to control her, even from the grave.

"You know I was his lawyer."

Iliya snorted. "Is that what you call it?"

With the scorn in her voice, Morena had no doubt Richard had been privy to at least some of William's playtimes starring Iliya. Richard was a good man but easily led. What had he done to her, under William's guidance?

Richard ignored Iliya's tone. "I'm looking after his will."

Morena gave a hiss of frustration. "He only passed away a few days ago. Surely you aren't ripping apart his estate yet?"

"William Burgess was a powerful man in the business world, with companies under his control that need to be stable to keep running." He grinned ruefully at them. "We've got our work cut out for us."

"We?" Iliya echoed.

"Yes. That's why I'm here rather than downstairs trying my hand at that adorable Gemma. I'm one of the executors of his will. Other than bequests to staff, and some long-lost nephew I've never heard of, he left everything to the two of you. With William's death, the two of you are very wealthy women."

CHAPTER THIRTY-ONE

Lorde

W HEN THE TREE WAS finally finished, as well as the eggnog and most of the champagne, Lorde found himself beside Tia at dinner.

"It's nice to finally meet Elizabeth," Tia began, draping her napkin on her lap. "Morena has told me so much about her. She's lovely."

"I like her," Lorde said gruffly. While he might love Elizabeth with all of his heart, body, and soul, it still didn't make it easy to talk about. Lorde found it difficult to express his feelings about life in general and almost impossible to talk about his love for Elizabeth.

Tia hid her smile behind her glass of wine, the ruby colour matching her lips. "I see that you do."

Lorde was content to let the conversation at the table swirl around him. He watched Elizabeth like always, covert glances mainly to reassure himself that she was really there. There was no possession in his gaze, only pride and if anyone looked closely, a mixture of joy and relief that she was really his.

Tia spoke to everyone around her, giving her full attention with her easy smile. She was a headmistress of an exclusive private school in Ontario, so dinners like this would be part of the job, Lorde decided. She was used to dealing with every walk of life, from entitled, snot-nosed kids to those scraped off the streets by the generosity and luck of a scholarship.

Coulter would have been one of those snot-nosed brats, Lorde thought to himself. There was something about the man that rubbed him the wrong way, in his expensive clothes and shiny shoes. He was surprised to see him and Jed laughing together. Morena had explained they were old friends, but Lorde couldn't see the connection. Jed was down-to-earth, a farmer with a laid-back attitude and easy smile. Coulter was a city slicker with a wariness in his eyes that he tried to hide with those toothpaste smiles.

It was the dimples. Lorde couldn't trust anyone with dimples that deep.

"What's troubling you, Michael?" Tia asked gently as Erin and Eric brought in the salads and began to serve.

Lorde didn't correct Tia on the use of his first name only because she was such a good friend of Morena's. Only Morena and Elizabeth were allowed to call him Michael.

His mother had called him Michael, and he wanted no reminders of her tonight or any other night.

"Nothing."

He wasn't about to tell Tia how he pictured Elizabeth and Coulter together, and the image felt like a vat of acid had been spilling on his insides. Elizabeth was curious. He knew that. He didn't like that, but he knew her interest in weekends like this was because she had a curiousity that wasn't being sated by him alone.

Lorde could satisfy her completely, but she wanted more. She wanted to even the score, although no one should be keeping track.

"How are Elizabeth's children adjusting?" Tia asked.

Lorde felt his face soften at the question. "Great. Good. They're both amazing girls."

"You love them."

"I don't know how anyone could help it. It's the only thing I admire about her arse of an ex-husband–that he helped create those two angels."

"Angels. You are smitten."

"I love them more than life itself," he said, surprising himself by his admission.

"Do you think you and Elizabeth might have more children?"

"We've...talked about it."

"Talking's a good first start."

"Actually..." Lorde leaned closer. A noisy dinner table wasn't his first choice for a conversation of this nature, but he didn't have a choice. "Elizabeth would like to have another baby, but there are a few things she wants to do first."

"Divorce her husband, I would imagine," Tia said.

"That's already in the works. And so far, so good. He knows it's best for her and the girls to be with me." Lorde didn't intend to sound threatening, but it often just happened when he talked about Alan. "No, it's a little different." He lowered his voice, dropping his chin to his neck. "Elizabeth isn't that...experienced."

Tia raised her eyebrows but said nothing.

"These weekends have really shown her what she's missed out on. Not that she's missed anything, or needs to have these experiences because it's fine that she's only been with two men..." He trailed off with a miserable expression.

"I know what you mean," Tia said gently. "It's a common emotion for those who have gotten married early or found themselves late bloomers. I think our new friends Gemma and Jasper feel the same way. They love each other, but they're interested in what else is out there."

"That's how Elizabeth feels."

"What are you going to do about it? Because knowing you, Michael–Lorde," she corrected. "I know you wouldn't be eager for her to express her curiousity with another man."

"No," he said shortly. Lorde took a deep breath. Now only to ask. "But a woman..."

"Ah. She's curious about that too."

"Maybe more than men. Which is fine."

"I imagine it would be for you." Tia smiled gently at him.

Tia looked so poised and contained; her intelligence shone out of those catlike eyes but there was more to her than her outward appearance. Lorde would know; he'd had a very memorable night with Tia years ago, another with Tia and another woman.

Because of that, he knew Tia would be perfect for what he was asking.

"I want to invite another woman to be with us," he said in a rush. "I want you. I want it to be you."

Tia was older, experienced. She could show Elizabeth what she needed–to give her the knowledge and maybe the skill, plus she was attractive enough to arouse even a woman who'd had no other partner like that.

"Would you...?" Lorde trailed off, not knowing what else he could say to show Tia what he was asking.

"I'd like nothing more," Tia said.

CHAPTER THIRTY-TWO

Gemma

G EMMA SAT BESIDE COULTER, his hand resting on her leg under the table

He had fed her drinks as they decorated the tree, got her a plate of cookies so the alcohol wouldn't go to her head.

"I want you to remember every moment of tonight," he told her, those blue eyes gazing deep into hers. Like he was burrowing into her soul.

She'd never met a man more attractive. Dominic was good-looking in a friendly way, but Coulter looked like a sorority girl's wet dream, if sorority girls had such a thing. He looked like a football player, a fireman, and one of the contestants on *The Bachelorette*, all rolled into one.

Gemma couldn't take her eyes off of him.

She finally had to drag her attention away when Liliane sat beside her. "Having a good time, new girl?"

"Are we the only ones who haven't been here before?" She glanced around the table, turned a questioning glance back at Coulter.

"I've never been here." Coulter raised his glass and touched it to hers.

Liliane smiled knowingly. "Yes, but you know all the rules of the game."

"There are rules?" Gemma asked, turning from Liliane to Coulter.

"That it's just a game. This is fun. We don't let emotions get involved."

Gemma frowned. Was this too good to be true? Was there something she and Jasper had missed? "I don't understand."

Coulter's attention was diverted by Heidi on the other side of him and Liliane took the opportunity to lean closer to Gemma. "I see the way you look at him, and I don't blame you. He's a sexy one, a real pretty boy, but that's it."

"He's nice," Gemma protested and Liliane laughed.

"Of course he is. But he's only here for sex, same as you. You have to remember that, with all his sweet talk and trying to sweep you off your feet, Coulter only wants to get you into bed. And in the morning, you're going to be back with your cute little hubby, and he's going to move on to his next conquest."

"I'm just a conquest?" Gemma was surprised how much the revelation stung.

"Of course not. Not tonight. Tonight you mean everything to that boy. Have fun with him. If he looked at me half like he's looking at you, I'd jump in there and give him a tumble. But be smart about it. Think with that–" Liliane pointed to her lap. "–and not this." She touched her chest. "Much easier that way."

Gemma glanced at her own lap. "I don't know any of this."

"And isn't it fun figuring it out? I can remember my first few times; if it wasn't for Morena's advice, I'd have fallen head over heels in love with him. Such a charmer and he made me feel like I was the only girl in the room, even when I wasn't. But I realized soon enough that I didn't need to feel love to have fun with him. And actually, it was more fun when I didn't." She leaned even closer. "One of my favourite times was with a man I didn't even like." She grinned at Gemma. "Be smart. Don't think with your heart."

"Thank you," Gemma said tremulously.

Liliane brushed her lips with her own. "Such a pretty thing. You'll have to come back for another visit."

"I think I'll wait to see how the rest of this weekend goes first," Gemma said.

CHAPTER THIRTY-THREE

Morena

ORENA WATCHED AS THE guests left the table in pairs and groups.

Jasper was one of the first, led out of the room by a beaming Heidi and Iliya. Gemma blew him a kiss before turning her attention back to Coulter, but Morena was worried about Jasper. Taking on even one of those women would be a challenge to most men, but both of them? She hoped he was up for it.

Richard looked unhappy as Coulter and Gemma got up from the table together. Gemma wore a wildly excited expression on her pretty face, and Coulter gave Morena a wink. He held Gemma's hand as they left the table.

If it wasn't for their talk that morning, Morena would be more worried about Gemma than Jasper. But after getting to know Coulter a little better, she knew he would take care of Gemma.

Two by two, or three by three, the table emptied. Even Liliane found a partner, escaping with Eric the waiter and the last bottle of champagne.

It was only Dominic at the table. Jed had given Morena a rueful smile as he and Jacey had left.

Morena turned from watching Liliane and Eric to find Dominic watching her at the other end of the table. "I'm surprised you're the last one here," she said lightly.

"I'm not." The legs of his chair scraped against the hardwood floor as he pushed his chair back. "I was waiting for you."

"Were you?"

"If you'd be so inclined," he added with a bashful smile. "I was waiting for the right opportunity to present my case during dinner but couldn't see my chance." He moved down the table and stood beside her chair.

She'd always liked Dominic. He was attractive with his solid body and curly dark hair, playful and sweet. He was a good husband to Jacey.

Morena's face fell. "Is this because of Jacey and Jed?"

Dominic took her hand and helped her stand. "It's in spite of that, actually. Last night was one of the few times Jacey and I swapped with a couple. Both of us prefer to go off on our own. And I've always had a bit of a crush on you, Morena."

Morena smiled as she followed Dominic to the door.

CHAPTER THIRTY-FOUR

Lorde

B EING WITH TWO WOMEN was every man's fantasy, and Lorde had had the real thing more than he could count. At times, the women had played with him, two mouths, four hands until he couldn't help but drive into one and then the other.

Sometimes, he had pleasured one with his mouth, while the other pleasured him.

At times he had watched the women together before joining in.

But never had he watched like this–standing stock-still with a rock-hard cock, unsure of exactly what to do.

Tia took charge, as Lorde had known she could. That was why it had to be her, someone experienced, gentle, and knowing. For his first time with Elizabeth, it had to be special.

Like the first night after Elizabeth had left Alan and come to him. He had wanted to woo, to seduce, to take his time with her, to show Elizabeth how much he loved her.

Elizabeth hadn't wanted to woo, to be seduced. She'd wanted him to fuck her.

There was nothing he wouldn't do for her. Including organizing this with Tia, because Elizabeth wanted to know what it was like.

He didn't expect this.

Lorde held his breath as Tia helped Elizabeth lay down on the bed.

He didn't know what to expect from this; if he could hold on to his jealousy. Because it was jealousy that reared up as Tia slowly undressed Elizabeth.

Another person was touching Elizabeth. Lorde had suffered through years of imagining Alan's slathering body crouched over his Elizabeth, and it had just about killed him.

And now here he was, allowing Tia full access to the woman he was in love with.

He didn't expect it to be so...hot.

Lorde could tell from the tenseness in Elizabeth's body that she was nervous. But there was no mistaking the soft sighs and moans for anything but excitement. Pleasure. As Tia moved down Elizabeth's now naked form, kissing and touching and caressing every bit of it, Lorde grew hard as he watched.

He stood at the end of the bed and watched Tia making love to Elizabeth.

First with fingers–gently exploring, softly probing Elizabeth's heat until Elizabeth began to move; arching her hips, demanding more. She grabbed a fistful of sheet and Lorde wondered if that was to stop herself from pushing Tia's head deeper between her legs.

He'd never seen her look more beautiful–legs spread, with Tia curled up between them, body arched with pleasure. Eyes half-closed, lips parted and the sounds...

Elizabeth was usually vocal, but this, watching and listening while not being caught up in the moment, was new.

It was sexy as hell.

She cried out, and Lorde shifted in an effort to release the pressure in his pants.

"Lorde?" Tia murmured, lifting her head. It might be even more enjoyable if you and I–"

Lorde didn't need to be asked twice. Freeing his cock from his pants, he grabbed a condom and quickly had Tia on her knees, still with her mouth between Elizabeth's legs.

As he slid into Tia's wet warmth, he groaned aloud.

Elizabeth's eyes flashed open. "Are you–?" she stammered raising her head from the pillow.

"No, not if you don't–"

"Do it." She collapsed with a low cry. "Do it at the same time. I want to watch. I want to–oh my god, this feels so good."

Tia moaned, and Elizabeth let out a tiny shriek. "That–do that. Make her do that again, Michael. Please."

Lorde had no idea what he had done, but he thrust hard into Tia, gripping her hips tightly, while he stared at Elizabeth.

At Elizabeth, eyes closed, face full of pleasure, so close to coming.

Lorde thrust harder, Tia moaned and Elizabeth cried out again.

It wasn't going to take him long either.

She was so warm, so wet. Muscles clutched at him, pulled him deeper inside.

He reached around Tia to caress Elizabeth's breast, toying with her nipple, rosy red and hard to the touch.

As hard as his cock.

Chapter Thirty-Five

Gemma

"So why are you here?" Coulter asked after he shut the door to the cabin behind her.

Gemma's skin prickled as she heard the click of the lock. Not that she was afraid or nervous.

Maybe a little nervous.

"I thought it would be fun." Gemma tried to for offbeat, casual. Relaxed, even though that was the last thing she was.

She'd tensed up when Coulter had first touched her leg during dinner, and she hadn't relaxed one little bit.

"And are you having fun?" A lamp in the corner created shadows in the little cabin. It was smaller than where they had been last night. Gemma didn't care about the size, but she was glad it was a different cabin. Last night was...

She wouldn't soon forget it.

Tonight would be different, and honestly, she wasn't expecting much. Not because of Coulter but because she knew nothing would ever be better than yesterday. The hot tub, and Jacey, and Dominic...

"I am." Gemma watched as Coulter sat easily on the bed, right in the middle against the pile of pillows.

"Now, or were you having fun? Because you seem a bit nervous."

"I'm not nervous." Her voice was too high-pitched to be truthful.

"Good. Then come and sit down with me so I can get to know you."

"You want to get to know me?"

"Of course. I want to find out what makes you tick, what makes you giggle." That made her giggle, just enough to sit on the edge of the bed. "I won't bite, you know. Unless you want me to."

"Why are you here?" Gemma asked as she kicked off her shoes, drawing her legs under her for warmth. The walk from the inn had been quick but cold, especially on bare legs.

"You're cold."

"I'm fine."

"I don't understand people who don't accept that they're cold when their lips are blue. Gemma, you are cold. Come get under the blanket." Coulter pulled down the white duvet, patting it invitingly.

Another shiver convinced her it might be a good idea.

"But your dress." Coulter frowned. "You'll wrinkle it if you keep it on."

"Is this a way to get me undressed?"

"Oh, I'll be getting you undressed, don't you worry about that." Coulter's drawl dove straight between Gemma's legs.

Holding her breath, she stood before him. "Will you unzip it for me, please?"

"With pleasure."

How were his hands so warm? And how was it possible to unzip so slowly? It was a challenge for Gemma to stand still as Coulter ran a hand down her back.

It wasn't that she was afraid–she wanted him. She may be nervous about what was going to transpire between them, but that didn't mean she didn't want it to start to transpire.

Once the dress was undone, the fabric gaping at the back, Coulter slipped his fingers under the edges and began easing it down her arms. "You're getting goosebumps," he whispered against the back of her neck.

"I don't think that's because I'm cold," she said in a low voice.

"No? That's nice." His lips pressed against her shoulder. Was that his tongue? Gemma stifled the gasp, feeling the flash of heat between her legs. "Is that nice?" He drew his hand around her waist and pulled her against him, his mouth French kissing her bare shoulders.

"Yes," she sighed. "Very nice."

"Imagine what I can do with the rest of you." With a final kiss, Coulter drew away. "But let's get you warm first. Dress off, under the covers. Right now."

Gemma slipped out of her dress and handed it to Coulter as she slid under the covers, the sheets cool under her suddenly over-heated skin. She watched as he neatly placed her dress on the chair facing the bed. "Are you going to take off your clothes?"

"Do you want me to?"

Gemma shrugged. "It's only fair."

Coulter caught her gaze and held it as he began unbuttoning his shirt. Slowly. Did the man do anything quickly?

Gemma couldn't wait to find out.

Especially not if his body looked like that. She caught her breath as Coulter took off his shirt, toyed with the button on his pants. His chest was chiselled and smooth. Gemma stared for a long moment after Coulter had stepped out of his pants before she pulled down the blanket, inviting him.

"This is warmer," he murmured. He lay on his side, an arm propped under his head and looked at her. Gemma dragged her gaze away from his chest. "So. Why are you here? Because you thought it would be fun. Are you looking for more fun?"

"Who isn't?"

"Lots of people, actually. Some people are quite content being unhappy, never wanting to challenge themselves, never moving outside their comfort zone."

"Is this outside your comfort zone?" Gemma asked.

"No, I'm pretty comfortable." Coulter reached out and drew a finger where the blankets met her skin. "I like touching you."

With a hand on her shoulder, Coulter turned Gemma to face him, letting his hand slide to her face. "You're so beautiful."

"You're just saying that."

"I say a lot of things. And I mean every one of them." He kissed her then, softly, his lips barely brushing hers before pulling back. "I should have asked to kiss you."

"I think we've moved past asking for consent."

"I want you to remember me as a gentleman."

"Are you?" Gemma asked, her throat dry with anticipation.

Coulter gave her a wicked smile and kissed her again. This one lasted longer. Gemma wanted it to last forever. Never before had a kiss invaded her very core. She arched against him, wanting his body pressed against hers.

His hand curved over her breast, dipping into her lacy bra to roll her nipple between his fingers. A jolt of heat arrowed between her thighs.

Gemma stifled the whimper of disappointment as Coulter pulled away from her lips, but the whimper soon turned to delight as he kissed his way down to her breasts.

Somehow her bra was unhooked, sliding off her shoulder without Gemma realizing what was happening.

Anything could happen in the room and she wouldn't realize it, not when his mouth was tracing patterns on her breasts, when his lips fixed on her rosy red nipple and suckled. Not when his hand slid its way down her ribs, to her belly.

Coulter bit her nipple and Gemma gasped a scream.

He raised his head and looked at her with a sinful smile. "Too hard?"

"Ah...no..."

"I think you like it dirty. You look like such a good girl, with the hair and those eyes, but this...this body tells me you like it rough."

Gemma gasped as Coulter thrust his hand past the waistband of her panties and found her nub, already swollen and sensitive. He rubbed and she spread her legs, pushing at her lacy panties at the same time.

"These are pretty but they have to go," Coulter said. With a strong tug, the scrap of fabric on the side broke.

Gemma gasped. "You broke my underwear."

Coulter gazed at her like he was daring her to complain. Like he might punish her if she said another word.

Gemma bit her lip, breathing hard as he jumped off the bed, and yanked down the remaining fabric like it was offensive.

It was offensive. Gemma wanted nothing impeding Coulter.

"I need to taste you now."

He grasped her legs and pulled her down the bed, before flipping her over onto her stomach. Strong hands on her ass–kneading and stroking, dipping down between to find the wetness that beckoned.

He helped her onto her knees, still with hands all over her ass. And then without a word, his mouth found her pussy.

He licked and sucked. He used fingers and lips and tongue–oh, his tongue. He nipped at her clit, sending a rush of sensation flooding through her.

Coulter invaded. He plundered.

His tongue licked the length of her, lapping every inch, toying at her puckered rosebud, before starting over again, and again.

Gemma buried her face in the pillow as her cries became louder. She couldn't take it. She couldn't stand it. It felt so good and...

And Coulter stopped.

He lifted his head from between her legs and Gemma could have wept with disappointment. "Gemma?" he growled.

"Yes?" Her voice was shaky, no more than a squeak.

"I want to hear you."

"You–okay."

"I want you to be loud. Don't put your head in the pillow. I need to hear you enjoy this. Are you enjoying this?" His hand roamed her ass, warm and controlling.

"Yes," she whispered. Anything, if he would only keep going.

"Yes, what?" Suddenly his hand cracked against her ass, so quickly Gemma didn't know what had happened until a flame of pain made her gasp. "Is that okay?" His fingers dipped back between her legs, his thumb finding her clit.

"Yes." He'd slapped her. Spanked her.

Jasper had never tried that.

"Can I do it again?" Coulter asked in a low voice, his finger now thrusting inside her.

"Yes."

Instead, he returned to her pussy, licking and sucking, plunging his tongue, his fingers inside of her so that there was no part of her that Coulter didn't explore. Even her ass–first his tongue, then his finger, then his thumb was inside her most private part.

Jasper had never done that either.

This time when Gemma cried out, she turned her face to the side so Coulter could hear how much she was enjoying it.

"Good girl," he soothed his hand back on her ass. She only had a moment to enjoy his touch before he spanked her again, rubbing away the sting as he plundered her again with his tongue.

Again and again and again, until Gemma's cries were almost a continuous scream as Coulter brought her closer and closer to the edge until she was begging for release, begging for him to make her come.

"Please! Oh, god, don't stop!"

And he didn't, licking and sucking her nub, fingers everywhere until Gemma crashed over the edge with a scream.

She was still shaking when Coulter stood up and plunged inside of her.

Gemma gasped at the size, the swiftness, the animalness of his thrusts. It was like her orgasm wouldn't stop–couldn't stop–as he fucked her roughly, finger biting into her hips.

She pitched forward at the power of his hips and grabbed fistfuls of the covers to steady herself.

Another slap only added to the intensity. It had never been like with Jasper. Never had she felt this...her body craving more...reaching for it.

"I'm coming," she shrieked as she barrelled toward the edge once more.

Her body arched as she came, harder than before, her mouth open in a wordless scream, trailing off into panting gasps as she shivered and shook.

"You're fucking beautiful," Coulter grunted as with a groan that seemed to come from deep inside, emptied himself into her.

"Next time I'll be a little more gentle," he promised as she lay spent on the bed.

"Again?" she asked with a weak smile.

CHAPTER THIRTY-SIX

Morena

THERE WERE NO WORDS.

Once they got to the cabin, Morena turned to Dominic and began unbuttoning his shirt. She knew what she wanted, and she was about to take it.

But so was Dominic. When his shirt hung open, exposing the smooth skin with the smattering of dark hair, he drew Morena close so her body fit tight to his and then kissed her.

Gentle at first; soft kisses like polite chitchat over dinner and for a moment Morena wondered if she's made a mistake.

And then Dominic took matters into his own hands.

He shifted, running warm hands down her arms, twining his fingers with hers as his lips parted and his tongue darted into her mouth.

He kissed her so thoroughly that Morena's knees began to weaken.

Morena had always liked Dominic. Always thought he was attractive. But she'd always been mildly obsessed with Jacey, and so Dominic had become a mere sidekick to Jacey's adventures.

With that first kiss, Dominic made the leap from sidekick accessory to leading man status.

He released her fingers to slide a hand around her head to deepen the kiss, his tongue tangling with hers. Morena held his shoulders, her hand in his curls. A soft noise escaped as Dominic began walking her backwards.

The bed hit the backs of her legs.

And then they were lying on the bed, with both still fully dressed. Lips, tongues, hands beginning to wander. They lay on the bed for long minutes, touching like frantic teenagers afraid of getting caught by parents.

Dominic's hand slid under her dress, smoothing her bare skin, sliding off her satin panties with a quick movement. Morena thought of stopping things, to take a moment to undress, but she didn't want to spoil the moment. Didn't want to stop when Dominic's fingers were doing such delicious things to her.

She kissed him on and on, even as she cried out against his mouth, hips thrusting against his hand.

And then his hand was gone, but his cock was there, pushing against her, and she spread her legs, wanting him inside her, wanting him now, not willing to stop and take a moment. He moved inside her, they moved together; slowly at first until they found their rhythm and then Dominic took control.

He tucked his hands under her, buried his face in the side of her neck as Morena's cries rang out into the quiet room.

CHAPTER THIRTY-SEVEN

Lorde

I T WASN'T UNTIL LORDE and Elizabeth were back at the house that he found the words to speak.

"Is that what you wanted?"

"I wanted..." Elizabeth stood by the end of the bed, still in her dress. "I didn't know I wanted that. I didn't know what to expect."

"I thought Tia..." he began gruffly.

"You'd been with her before?"

"Once. Long ago. Not like that."

"Was it... Was it okay for you?" she asked, her voice soft. Lorde only shook his head. "Was it?"

"You have to ask?"

With a smile, Elizabeth slid off her dress, replaced it with a night-gown before pulling back the covers. "Did you like it?"

"What do you think?"

"What about seeing me with Tia?"

Lorde followed her into bed, fighting the urge to take her in his arms again. "Do you really want a recap?"

"I do. I'll tell you anything you want to know."

"I don't know what I want to know."

"Do you want to know that as exciting as that was, it's still better with you. Just you...and me."

Lorde dropped his eyes. That was exactly what he wanted to know.

"Do you want to know there was nothing sexier than having you make love to me last night? Tia was–Tia is–amazing. Really. I've never been with a woman before. It was new."

"And..." Lorde prompted.

"And it was exciting and sexy and it felt really good. But it doesn't mean it was better than you."

"I'm not asking that?"

"No? You're a man, Michael, but that doesn't mean you still can't be a little insecure after you've watched a woman give me two orgasms."

"Two?" Lorde's stomach sank. "I thought it was just one."

"Two. The first one was so quick but the second..." Elizabeth grinned mischievously. "Want to see if you can make it three?"

"You're incorrigible," Lorde grumbled as he rolled on top of her.

"And you love it."

"I love you," he said against her lips.

"And I love you too. Just you. But I might want to try something like that again."

"We'll talk about it later." Lorde began kissing his way down her body. "After I finish three."

Elizabeth gasped with delight as Lorde disappeared under the covers.

CHAPTER THIRTY-EIGHT

Gemma

GEMMA STILL WORE THE thick robe when the knock
sounded on the door. Jasper had already gone down to
breakfast, after waking up ravenously hungry.

Gemma would have been concerned had he not already made
love to her before he left.

It had been different from what it had been with Coulter because the two men were nothing alike. Jasper was quieter and
reserved than Coulter with all his laid-back charm.

She opened the door to find Jacey standing there.

"I saw Jasper go down but not you so I came to check in," she
said, brushing past Gemma without waiting for an invitation to
come in.

"I was going to get dressed and..." Gemma stared as Jacey
perched on the bed, sheets still sleep rumpled.

"I won't be long. Morena's breakfasts are my second favourite
thing about this place."

"What's your favourite?" Gemma asked. Jacey cocked her head and raised her eyebrows. "Oh. Right. The sex?"

"The sex with other people," Jacey agreed. "Not that I don't do that at home, but it's nice to have a bit more variety."

"You really...you're in a group of swingers?"

"I wouldn't call them a group...there are about five couples and Tia, and sometimes Tia has friends. And we swap."

"Wow. How often does this happen? All at once or one at a time?" Now that Jacey was here and talking, Gemma didn't know what to ask her first. "And your marriage? It seems fine but–"

"It is fine. My marriage is great. Dominic understands I need a little extra sex. And he gets to do it too, but it's kind of more for me. We've decided I have a very healthy libido."

"Healthy libido," Gemma repeated.

"You should meet my friend Melissa. I think she wants it more than I do. Her husband..." Jacey trailed off with a shiver. "Unbelievable."

"He's that good?"

"His tongue."

"Ah." Gemma wondered what an unbelievable tongue was like. Was it better than Coulter?

She couldn't stop the stirring between her legs.

That was why she didn't rush down to the kitchen with Jasper. They were leaving today, never to see these people again.

Jacey and Dominic, Coulter and even Morena had changed her world, and Gemma needed a few minutes to figure out what that meant. Was this going to be a one-time thing? Would it be ongoing for her and Jasper? Maybe they could make it a yearly event.

But deep down, Gemma knew that as much as she loved Jasper, she wasn't going to be able to handle a one-time thing, or even yearly.

She wanted more.

"I hope you meet them." Jacey paused. "That's why I'm here. We were wondering if you and Jasper would like to come to one of Tia's parties."

"Her key parties?"

Jacey nodded. "The others would love you. Tia and I were talking about it yesterday. She wasn't sure you would be into it, but after the first night..." Jacey gave Gemma a catlike smile.

"Really?"

"Really. I think it'd be fun. You said you wanted excitement. This is pretty tame compared to a few of the clubs out there."

Gemma shook her head. "Oh, I couldn't do that."

"You'd be surprised what you could do. Did you ever think you'd spend the weekend at a swinger resort?"

"Not really, no."

"Well, then." She stood up. "I'm going to get some of that French toast before it's all gone. I wanted to ask you about this first. Think about it."

"I will."

As she closed the door behind Jacey, Gemma knew she would be thinking of nothing else.

CHAPTER THIRTY-NINE

Morena

MORENA WAVED AS THE final car drove away, and then sighed.

Another successful weekend. This one was more emotional than usual. And Morena knew it wasn't just William's death. She hadn't even touched on the emotions she felt, especially learning William had left everything to her and Iliya. It made her feel guilty, but she wasn't sure why. And Morena couldn't deny the relief the thought of what the money could do for her. No more worries about the inn.

But it was more than that. Having Coulter here made things different with Jed. Having Jed take part made things different.

Morena wasn't sure how she felt about that.

She'd enjoyed herself with Dominic last night, but knew she didn't need him. She would have been content to end her evening after dinner.

The thought of Jed with Jacey wriggled at her subconscious like a worm burrowing into the dirt.

Jacey and Jed had sex, just like she and Dominic had. And Morena didn't begrudge Jed or Jacey for it, but she wished she had an easier time accepting it.

As she turned into the house, Morena heard the sound of an approaching car. It was a moment before she recognized Jed's truck.

She waited on the porch for him. Jed had left soon after lunch with Coulter, taking him back to his house where Coulter was spending a few days.

Morena wasn't sure what she thought about Coulter being under the same roof as Jed. Knowing the two had been together caused mixed emotions. Jealousy, as well as a bit of arousal. The sight of the two men kissing had been a bigger turn-on than Morena had realized it would be.

But...

Morena didn't want to share Jed. Not with Coulter, not with Jacey. She wanted him all to herself.

The realization sank like a stone to the pit of her stomach as Jed stepped from the truck.

He was so beautiful, so long and lean, and fun. Fun to be with, fun to play with. And so young.

"Everyone leave you?" Jed called as he loped up the stairs.

"I think that's a good thing." She sighed.

"Even me?" His arms circled her waist automatically and Morena leaned against him without being conscious of it. They fit together so naturally, so nicely. The age difference wasn't a big thing when Jed was holding her.

She loved him holding her.

She loved him.

"Never you," she said in a low voice.

"It was a good time," Jed said, dropping a kiss on the top of her head. "Coulter kept talking about coming back for another weekend."

"He is…" She wasn't sure what she thought of Coulter. Like a puppy? Like a sexy movie star, women dreamt about? Like an amazing man who held a piece of Jed's heart?

"He is that," Jed agreed to her unspoken comments. "I hope you liked him."

"I adore him. It's hard not to," she admitted. "What about you?"

Jed pulled away enough to meet her gaze. "I'm sorry I didn't tell you about him. We haven't talked a lot about our past. I thought that's what you wanted."

"I'm not sure what I want."

"What's that supposed to mean?" Jed asked quickly with a worried frown.

"I don't know—Oh, no! Nothing like that." Morena was quick to reassure him. "I want you. I want you all the time." She swallowed her fear, her uncertainties. "I love you, Jed."

Jed's smile was brighter than the afternoon sun beating down on them. "You do, do you?"

"I know you've already said it to me."

"I was waiting until you were ready. I don't mind waiting, especially not for you."

"You shouldn't have to. This age thing just gets in my head."

"What age thing?" Jed asked innocently and Morena laughed.

"Just wait another couple of years until I'm getting a pension."

"It only means you can get cheaper movie tickets when I take you out. Seniors discount you know."

Morena slapped his shoulder and Jed laughed as he hugged her closer. "I love you Morena Raspillaire, however old you may be. And however old you get won't change things either."

For once Morena decided not to agree, but to believe what Jed was saying.

"I was thinking about Coulter," she hedged.

"Good or bad or dirty?"

"It was...fun with him," Morena began.

"I thought you did have fun, but right now it doesn't really sound like it."

"I did...but..."

"There's that but. Look, Morena, that can be a one-time thing. Coulter doesn't have to come to visit again, or if he does, we can keep it out of the bedroom. He's my friend, and we've had a few laughs, but it doesn't mean I'm pining for him."

"Are you sure? Because if that's something you want–?"

"I want you to stop trying to make everyone happy, and start being selfish," Jed said. "If you don't want to be with Coulter again, we won't."

"I don't want to be with anyone," Morena said in a rush.

"What?"

"Anyone else. I only want to be with you, Jed. These weekends are fun, but now I have you–now that I love you, I don't want–I want it to just be the two of us. No sharing."

Morena held her breath as Jed looked at her searchingly. "I can handle that."

"If it's not what you want..."

"I want you," Jed interrupted, his fingers pressed against her lips. "However you want me. If it's only to be me and you, so much better."

He kissed her then as they stood on the porch, the kiss warming Morena even more than the sun.

The End

Want more Gemma?
Check out
Fantasies Book Club!

Hello readers!

I hope you've enjoyed the fourth book in my Adults Only series! Thanks so much for sticking with me. I love my readers and I love your support. I'd love to hear from you – visit my website and let me know you finished and what you think. And leave a review where ever you bought this! It's so important for authors to have reviews!

Love to you all,

Anna

xo

www.AnnaEllis.ca

Anna Ellis likes to write about happily married couples having sex with other happily married couples. There's no werewolves or vampires, shapeshifters or tentacles involved - just good, old-fashioned sex. And maybe a little tying up. Or a spanking or two.

In the **Husbands and Wives** series, follow new neighbours Jacey and Dominic as they learn to navigate the slippery sidewalks of suburban swinger lifestyle. Being a good neighbour has never been so much fun!

Her new series, **One**, returns to the swinger lifestyle with three married couples looking to spice up their marriages. One Summer, One Week, and One Night, all coming soon!

Her **Office Plays** series takes you to the workplace to meet the most excitable group of office employees you would ever want to work with. They give coffee breaks a new meaning.

The series **Touch** is an unconventional love story about a woman who falls in love with a man...and his wife. All nine books are available now, *Touch*, *Caress,* and *Embrace.* Each has three separate points of view from Kenna, Iliya, and Del.

Adults Only follows Morena and Lorde, who run a B&B especially for swingers. The four-book series includes characters from other series—Jacey and Dominic from **Husbands and Wives**, Callie, from **Office Plays**, and Iliya from **Touch**. While you don't need to read the other series first, it would improve your pleasure!

And her latest series, **Fantasies Book Club,** brings back a few favourites as a book club reads dirty stories that seem to mirror their own lives.

Anna also writes women's fiction/chick lit under the name Holly Kerr. If you're looking for something a little less steamy (but still hot!) check out her books.www.hollykerr.ca

Visit Anna at or Facebook
Or visit Holly at
They'd love to hear from you!!
Happy Reading!

Also By Anna Ellis

Husbands and Wives series
Making Friends
The Husbands
The Wives
New Neighbours
Joe and Jacey
Husbands and Wives—The Collection
Interludes
Interludes II
Interludes III
Interludes—The Collection
Melissa
Paige

Touch series
Touch
Touch—Iliya's Story

Touch—Del's Story

Caress

Caress—Iliya's Story

Caress—Del's Story

Embrace

Embrace—Iliya's Story

Embrace—Del's Story

Office Plays series

Office

Plays

Secrets and Lies

Love After Hours

Lost Weekends

Adults Only series

Shared Accommodations

Room Service

Late Check Out

No Vacancy

One series

One Summer

One Week

One Night

Fantasies Book Club

Gemma

Emmy

Callie

Nia

Malcolm

Short story collection

Peek-a-boo

Made in the USA
Columbia, SC
06 December 2024

48594464R00120